SIGN OF THE DOVE

OTHER BOOKS BY

SUSAN FLETCHER

THE DRAGON CHRONICLES:

Dragon's Milk

Flight of the Dragon Kyn

Alphabet of Dreams

Shadow Spinner

Walk Across the Sea

SIGN OF THE DOVE

SUSAN FLETCHER

ATHENEUM BOOKS FOR YOUNG READERS
NEW YORK . LONDON . TORONTO . SYDNEY

ATHENEUM BOOKS FOR YOUNG READERS
An imprint of Simon & Schuster Children's Publishing Division
1230 Avenue of the Americas, New York, New York 10020

The text for this book is set in Garamond.
Manufactured in the United States of America
0210 MTN
First Atheneum Books for Young Readers paperback edition March 2010
2 4 6 8 10 9 7 5 3 1
The Library of Congress has cataloged the hardcover edition as follows:
Fletcher, Susan, 1951–
Flight of the Dragon Kyn / Susan Fletcher.
p. cm.
"A Jean Karl book."
Summary: As the last of the dragon eggs, laid long ago, begin to hatch, Lyf becomes a reluctant friend who tries to save both the dragon mothers and their newly born children from their enemies.
ISBN 978-0-689-80460-1 [hc]
[1. Dragons—Fiction. 2. Fantasy.] I. Title.
PZ7.F6356 Si 1996
[Fic]—dc20
95000584
ISBN 978-1-4169-9714-6 [pbk]
ISBN 978-1-4424-0973-6 [eBook]

For all of my rescuers,
and especially Gervaise Sadowski,
Ann Vess, Theresa Johnson,
Becky Huntting, Ann Missal,
Rinda Kilgore, and Kay Stevenson.

ACKNOWLEDGMENTS

I am grateful for the generous help of Will Earhart,
Annie Callan, Lois Dowey, and Sue Schoenfeld.
Many thanks to my writers' groups for all the stories.
And special thanks to Jean Karl,
for befriending and nurturing my dragons.

Harper's Tale

Long ago, my lords and ladies, before the time of your mothers' mothers' mothers, dragons flourished upon the earth. They flew unfettered over the great green forests. They laired serenely in the high mountain crags. Their prey were the deer and the foxes and the bears.

They preyed also on *humans*, you say?

Only as a cornered wolf preys upon its hunter, my lord.

Humankind began to multiply and cover the earth, encroaching upon the Ancient Ones' domain. Many a clash rang out between men and dragons. Sometimes men prevailed, and sometimes dragons. But humans, growing in numbers and in power, triumphed more and more.

Year by year, the Ancient Ones moved north, away from the lands of humans. Yet soon there were no safe places to lair, even in the far, far north of this land. The dragons' numbers dwindled, until the survival of their kyn was at peril.

And so the dragons, aided by Kara Dragon-sayer, took flight for an unknown land far across the Northern Sea. The Migration, folk called it. To this day no one knows for certain where the land of dragons lies.

But that is another tale for another night, my lords and ladies.

This night I will tell of a girl called Lyf.

Chapter 1

The Dove

Lyf looked out across the graze to the wood beyond, searching.

Mist lay heavy in the air, thick as cream where it scudded across the ground, dissolving to a thin, smoky haze higher up.

She had sensed something moments before. A quick fluttering-across-the-mind. The reed-thin thread of a pulse.

It was a bird—that much she knew.

Often she had felt them—birds—but she quickly pulled away. She was forbidden to ken with birds. She was afraid to ken with birds, because of the time when the blackness had come.

And yet this one had the feel of a message-dove, the way it grew near and purposefully nearer. Perhaps it had come from Kaeldra. Lyf longed to have word from Kaeldra.

The damp air gusted chill upon Lyf's neck. She wrapped her cloak more tightly about her and gazed at the stark profiles of the trees. They floated silent above the fog, their black branches lightly misted with green. Farther back, they faded to gray and lighter gray, melting at last to mere ghosts of trees, bleached to the color of fog.

There. Above them now. The dove.

Lyf did not touch it with her mind, but waded through the wet, matted grass to the dovecote. She was forbidden to go near the doves. But Granmyr had gone to her garden, and Mama and Mirym were working high in the graze with the lambs. None would know. She would not ken with this dove but only look, only see if it were banded. Then someone else could fetch it.

And now she heard the creaking of wings; she turned to watch. A message-dove it was, pumping hard for the cote. And though she had not meant to do it, Lyf weakened and called to it in the kenning way. She touched the birdness with her mind, felt it veer toward her. The dove pitched up, alighted on her wrist. She felt its bloodbeat merging with her own—then wrenched her mind away.

Lyf teased up the feathers of the dove's soft breast. It stretched one gray-and-white wing, then burbled and pecked at its feet. And there she saw it: a rolled-up strip of vellum, tied to the scaly red leg.

Now Lyf did not know what to do. If she read the missive and then gave it to Mama and Granmyr, they would scold her for meddling with the birds. But she did not want to wait. She wanted to see it *now*. She could run and tell Granmyr, but one never knew with Granmyr—she might keep the news to herself.

Lyf was still hesitating when a new sound came to her through the fog: a beating of many hooves. Not light and crisp like sheep hooves or goat hooves. Not slow and plodding like mule hooves. No, these came heavy and hard and fast.

Horse hooves.

She peered through the drifting mist, but could see nothing.

"Lyf! To the cottage! Now!" And Granmyr was shouting at her, was running round the corner of the cottage.

Lyf thrust the dove deep inside the folds of her kirtle, hoping Granmyr had not spied it. Not a word did the old woman utter, but only gripped Lyf's arm at the elbow and hurried her through the grass and into the cottage. Granmyr bent down, swept away a patch of strew-reeds, tugged at the root cellar hatch.

"Get you within," she said when she had pried it up, "and shush! I will tell you when it's safe."

In the cellar? "But why? I—"

"Within!" And Granmyr was pushing her down.

Lyf groped from rung to rung down the ladder and at last felt the hard-packed floor beneath her. The light above narrowed to a sliver, then vanished. All dark. Granmyr's footsteps echoed hollowly overhead.

Lyf was alone.

Her heart beat wildly in her throat. She gulped in a deep breath; the sweet smells of roots mingled with the sharp, musty tang of mildewed reeds. The cool, still air felt clammy on her skin.

What was it Granmyr had said? *I will tell you when it's safe.*

Safe from what?

Lyf laid a hand over the dove, where it rested between her kirtle and her shift. Its heartbeat pulsed in her palm.

"There," she said, more to comfort herself than the bird. "All's well."

But all was *not* well. It was dark and close and fearsome down here all alone. And something was wrong . . . the horses. . . . Who had come riding horses?

Lyf coaxed the dove out from beneath her kirtle and cupped it in one hand against her chest. She fumbled for the message, then picked at the string until the scrap of vellum came free. She wished she could see to read it. Perhaps it held some clue. Lyf tucked the vellum securely into her sash. If the message were lost, Granmyr would be doubly vexed. Lyf didn't think that Granmyr had seen the bird; she would have said something if she had. She would have taken it away. But now Lyf would have to own up to what she had done. When she got out. *When it was safe*.

She started, as a sudden loud banging came from above. Then voices—harsh and guttural. Kragish voices. Soldiers' voices.

"She is not here," Lyf heard Granmyr say. "She has gone with her husband to trade horses in the eastern lands. They have put out their farm to lease."

Kaeldra. They were asking after Kaeldra.

One man said something—"Move aside!" Lyf thought she heard. Then came the tramp of many boots upon the floor. She heard a creak and a scraping noise, and then there were other voices—Mama's and Mirym's. There was talking to and fro among them, but Lyf could not make out the sense of it because the footfalls on the wooden door above drowned out their words. She caught fragments only: *tall* and *straw-colored hair* and *green eyes*. And then one of the Krags said something—it went up at the end, like a question—and there was a moment when no one spoke.

"Lyf is with Kaeldra." Granmyr's voice came with surprising clarity, directly above, and at the same time Mama said, "Lyf? Who is Lyf?"

Silence again—deep silence. Lyf's heart was thudding so hard, it seemed that they must hear it. The dove struggled sharply, then burst out with a loud *coo coo coo*.

"What was that?" The Krag's voice was sharp. Then other voices—all at once—broke in. Lyf shrank back. She heard footsteps and a scrabbling noise overhead. They were searching for the cellar hatch. They were searching for *her*.

Lyf thrust the dove back inside her kirtle, scrambling blindly backward over sacks of grain and baskets of roots and sheaves of reeds. She clambered into an empty basket and crouched down within. A crack of light appeared above, widening. . . .They were coming. She grabbed for a sheaf of reeds and pulled it atop her. Then another and another, until she was covered with a thick, reedy thatch.

And now she heard a boot clunk down on a ladder rung.

"A light! That candle—give it to me!" The voice sounded loud, sounded near.

Lyf's heart pounded in her throat. She could feel the bird growing restless in her hands. *Hush*, she willed. *Hush!*

At the edges of her eyes she saw a yellow, wavery light. Lyf hunched down inside the basket, listened to the boots clunking down. And then he was with her in the cellar. She could feel the heat from his body; she could smell his sweat.

Lyf held her breath, *willed* the dove to be still.

Hush.

It was going to coo. She touched the birdness with her mind and she felt the cooing coming on.

Hush.

She heard the man's boots grating in the dirt. He was

walking, but not far; he stayed in the cleared-out patch near the ladder. The light at the edges of her eyes grew brighter, and then dimmer.

"Is she there?" came a voice from above.

"No. There's no one here. Likely it was a rat we heard, or the wind."

The light flickered, and Lyf heard a boot thunk against wood. The ladder. He was climbing up the ladder. Slowly, she let out her breath.

The dove rustled its feathers, loud as thunder in Lyf's ears.

Hush.

Silence. Then footfalls, coming back down. Crossing the dirt floor. Coming toward *her*. Light flared to one side of her; Lyf held herself still as stone.

Breathing. She could hear him breathing. He did not move.

The bird was restless, restless. It was going to coo; she could feel it. It struggled in her hands; she held it tight.

"Do you see her?" The voice from above.

"I don't know," the man said, and he was close—so close. "There is something. . . ."

Coo. The bird wanted to coo, but Lyf wouldn't let it. She went all the way down inside it, felt the birdness close in around her. The cellar smells surged in, suddenly bright: grain, reeds, roots, candle wax, man. She could hear the wind stirring in the thatch; she could hear insects scurrying in the reeds. And beneath it all ran a low, throbbing hum, a pulsing of blood.

Hush! she willed. *Hush.* And then the words fell away from her, and the *pulse pulse pulse* of the bird's heart merged with her own.

Harper's Tale

Dragon eggs, my lords and ladies, must ripen for a hundred years before the hatching. Or *nearly* a hundred years. They are all laid in the spring of the selfsame year—but some ripen early and some late, so there is a seven-year span of hatching for each new generation.

In the Migration, the dragons had to leave their eggs behind. But the Ancient Ones cherish their young, my ladies —much as we.

And so, when their eggs began to hatch, the dragon dams returned.

They did not find the land as they had left it. It was grown more crowded with humans, who were grown more cunning in weaponry. Many dragon dams, unable to fly while nursing, were slain. And their hatchlings, as well.

And then the queen put out the wolf's head—to make matters worse.

It looked to be the end of all the new generation of dragons.

But I have not yet told of Lyf, you say?

I will come to her soon enough.

Patience, my lady, is a virtue.

CHAPTER 2

Kymo

Light pressed heavy on Lyf's face. A harsh, acrid smell filled her nose, made her gasp for breath. She opened her eyes; the light hurt. She shut them again.

"The bitters are taking. She wakes."

Granmyr's voice. It sounded muted, distant, as though Lyf were hearing it from deep under water. Far above came the sound of wings slapping. Again Lyf opened her eyes, and saw feathers rocking down through the light.

Lyf forced her awareness up toward the voice. Slowly, she sat up. The acrid stench receded; the smells of reeds and roots hung thick in the air. She was in the cellar. Granmyr stooped over her with a candle. Mama, kneeling at her side, let out a soft sob and clutched Lyf to her. Her kirtle felt scratchy on Lyf's cheek. Then, "You were not to go near those doves!" she said.

"Hush," Granmyr said. "Not now. Help her up." Mama reached out her hands; Lyf took them and pulled herself to her feet.

It was wobbly, on her feet. Lyf picked her way through the wavering shadows, among the sacks of grain and baskets of roots. Once, her legs nearly buckled, but she caught herself in time. Granmyr guided her to the ladder, motioned her up.

Dizzy. She felt dizzy.

She held on tight to the ladder and climbed, moving each foot carefully up before setting her weight down upon it. And then Mirym—her grown-up sister Mirym—was hauling her up through the hatch and onto the cottage floor. She helped Lyf to her feet, led her to sit on a bench.

That man. Lyf remembered now: the Krag searching for her in the cellar. "What happened to that Krag?"

"He left," Mirym said, "with the others. Granmyr started plaguing them; you know how she can do. . . ."

Lyf smiled despite herself. She *did* know. Granmyr was small and reed-thin, but Lyf had seen many grown men sputter and turn crimson before the old woman's piercing gaze.

". . . and then you didn't answer when we called down to you."

Because of the blackness. She had gone down inside the bird mind to make it hush, and after that the blackness had come.

For as long as she could remember, Lyf had known how to touch a bird mind with her own. She did so as you would touch a hot kettle with a finger, snapping it back quickly so as not to get burned. She could summon birds that way, though it was forbidden. She had summoned *this* bird that way.

But she could get lost inside a bird if she went down too

deep. *Had* done so once before, when she was younger. She had swooned upon the forest floor, and only smelling bitters had revived her. And so she was forbidden.

Lyf sat listening as Granmyr and Mama climbed up from the cellar and Mirym busied herself at the hearth. "You know we must," Granmyr was saying. "The soldiers will return, never doubt it. They'll be seeking her out. She's no longer safe here, or anywhere hereabouts."

"It's *Kaeldra* they want," Mama retorted. "Her and that Kragish husband of hers. Oh, I could throttle her for dragging Lyf into this. Before *she* came, Lyf was not—" She stopped and glanced at Lyf.

"Kaeldra saved the child's life, remember you, daughter," Granmyr said. "With dragon's milk. And the green of Lyf's eyes is the price of her saving. We owe Kaeldra for that. And the dragons."

Kaeldra, Lyf thought. There was something she must remember, of Kaeldra. . . .

"But how if they pursue her?" Mama said. "How if she must live in hiding all her life long?" Her voice rose in its habitual whine, and Lyf felt the familiar tightening of fear at her throat. The danger might never pass. The soldiers would come after her; no place would be safe. . . .

"Bletherchaff!" Granmyr's voice cut in. "This *will* pass; the hatchings are nearly done. We all suffer from this trouble—not Lyf only. Mirym is divided from her husband, Kaeldra from her daughters and her home. Soon the dragons will fly from our land back to their home over the Northern Sea. Then there will be no need to get into such a ferment over folk with green eyes. Then all can be united. Meantime, Kaeldra will welcome another pair of strong hands."

"Strong! Lyf is not strong! Never has she been strong—not since she was taken with the fever. And she hasn't the sense to leave off meddling with birds. Not yet twelve winters old, and small for her years at that. And frail—she is frail. . . ."

Birds. Lyf came back now to the dove. There had been a message. . . . Lyf fumbled in her sash and found it. "The dove . . . it bore this," she said.

Mama reached for it, but Granmyr's hand was quicker. She snatched it from Lyf and read it silently. There were many marks on the vellum—Lyf could see that. Few folk in Elythia were schooled in letters, so most message doves bore only metal bands inked with the marks of their senders. But Granmyr could read—as could Lyf—for Kaeldra's husband, Jeorg, had taught them.

Granmyr's lips pursed hard. She tucked the message into her sash.

"What news?" Mirym asked. "Is there word of my husband?"

Granmyr merely shook her head. "Best you know nothing of this—then none may pry it from you. But now we can kill two hares with the selfsame shaft, for the message is for Kaeldra, and Lyf can fetch it to her. She can go with the harper; I hear tell he's in Wyrmward now. We'll send for him."

"Oh, my Lyfling." Sobbing, Mama clutched Lyf to her, forcing her to stand. Lyf felt fear surging up inside. Going to Kaeldra and Jeorg, to their secret, far-off place. The perilous trek through the mountains. The soldiers seeking her. Lyf drew in a ragged, frightened breath, then caught Granmyr regarding her. Granmyr nodded gravely, as if to someone strong—as if *she* were stronger than Mama.

And Lyf felt something odd then: a prickling of excitement.

Perhaps she would see a dracling, help it escape. Long had she heard of draclings—from the time nearly seven summers past when Kaeldra had gone up the mountain and brought back the milk of a nursing dragon. It was for Lyf she had done it. Lyf had been taken with vermilion fever, and only dragon's milk could cure it.

It *had* cured the fever, though it had turned Lyf's eyes a rare and startling green. And ever since, Lyf had been able to do this odd thing that no one else could do: She could ken with birds. Granmyr had told her that long ago she had known another who could ken with birds. Yet with Lyf the kenning was different. Deeper. More perilous.

And now . . . to see a dracling . . . it would be an adventure.

But she was frail—from the fever. Mama always said so. She was allowed only to help with the least taxing work—none of the plowing or lambing or shearing. She was not strong enough for adventures.

"Best help her to the loft, now, to sleep," Granmyr said, "for this night she will get no rest. I'll send Mirym to fetch the harper. Then at darkfall, they will go."

Lyf did not think that she could sleep, and yet the kenning must have wearied her, for one moment she was listening to the voices below, and the next Granmyr was rousing her. And it all came back in a rush of dread—that she must leave her home where she had lived all her life to go into hiding, that she must trek through the dark forest with the harper, that the Kragish soldiers were seeking her out.

Granmyr helped her below, and there Lyf saw the harper straddling a bench, regaling Mirym and Mama with music and a tale. His harp gave out mood more than melody, echoing the tone of his voice. His words coursed along softly, then all at once he called out, *"Foom!"* Mirym giggled with delight; even Mama smiled. Kymo, this harper was called. Lyf minded him now. She had seen him a time or two before, at the market fair in town. She had fancied his tales, but had not stopped to consider *him*. Now she eyed him more carefully, taking in his stout but solid build, his wild thatch of blue-black hair. He looked to have thirty winters or thereabouts, with crinkly lines fanning out from the edges of his eyes and bracketing his wide mouth. His brown-gold eyes seemed to laugh even when his mouth did not. Something glinted on his chest in the firelight: a copper amulet, shaped like a dove. *Ah*, Lyf thought. He was of the dove sign. He was allied in Kaeldra's cause.

Mama rose and fetched Lyf's cloak; then she flung her arms about her. She peppered Lyf with warnings—about keeping herself warm, about taxing her strength, about kenning with birds. Then she burst into tears, moaning that Lyf was too frail, the trek too perilous.

Fear raced again through Lyf's veins; tears pricked at the backs of her eyes. It was hard, too hard; she *shouldn't* have to go.

And then Granmyr was thrusting something into her hand. "Hide this in your sash, Lyfling, and give it to Kaeldra when you arrive." It was the message from the dove. Lyf began to unfurl it, but Granmyr took it out of her hands and tucked it firmly into her sash. "Let Kaeldra read it first. Be of good use to her, little one. She has need of you. And no more kenning with birds. It is perilous, do you hear me? Each time you do it, the danger grows." Granmyr paused, brushed a wayward tear from Lyf's cheek. "There now. No call for that. You're stronger than you know."

Kymo's mule stood laden and waiting without. It was dark; mist flowed across a slice of moon. Lyf made her farewell to Mirym—a long, tearful hug. "Tell Nysien I miss him," Mirym said. "Tell him to come home soon."

Kymo boosted Lyf up onto his mule, then walked a little way ahead of the beast, tugging on its rope. The mule set its heels and began to pull backward. "Come along, Grumble. Come along." The mule made a rumbling noise deep in its throat and shook its head. Kymo sighed. "I'll be needin' your help now," he said to Lyf. "If you would only scratch inside her ear a bit—no, not that one, t'other." Lyf put her hand inside the mule's hairy left ear and timidly began to scratch. Grumble lurched forward all at once, throwing Lyf sharply back. She grabbed for the bristly mane and held on with all her might. Kymo, she saw, was sprinting ahead so as not to be trampled. Soon, Grumble eased into a jarring trot; Lyf strove to reseat herself in the tight space between the baggage and the mule's neck.

When at last Grumble had slowed to a walk and Lyf turned round to wave farewell, Granmyr and Mama and Mirym were but shadows in the mist.

Harper's Tale

What wolf's head, you ask, my lord?

Did not your mother tell you? Your father?

No?

Ah, you young folk today know nothing of history!

I will tell it, then. Hark you well.

It happened that many years ago, near the end of the last span of hatching, there was a queen in Kragrom. Her cousin, the old king's sister's son, craved the throne for himself. And indeed, there were many who did not wish to be ruled by a woman. They banded with the queen's cousin and drove her out.

The queen and her minions lay low in the woods of Elythia, plotting her return. They got neither help nor hindrance from the Krags already living in this land. These preferred to wait, to see how the game played out. Neither did the new king pursue her, but shored up his defenses in Kragrom.

It had long been rumored that by eating a dragon's heart a man might protect himself against the bite of metal. The queen, believing this, sent her soldiers out searching, armed with the silver pipes whose tones were known to put dragons in a trance.

And just to be certain, she offered a reward. A wolf's head, as they called it.

Grown or young, alive or dead, it mattered not to her—so long as the dragons had hearts. She would build an army invulnerable to the sword.

And yet, my lords and ladies, the dragons were not friendless among men.

CHAPTER 3

An Adventure!

They struck out north, across the graze, avoiding the town altogether. Before long the cleared ground ended and the forest crowded in close. They made their way along narrow tracks, so deeply shaded and thick with drifting fog that at times Lyf could scarce see her hands before her.

Lyf would have been afraid—she *was* afraid—but Kymo kept up a steady stream of stories. He neither sang nor played his harp, but wore it slung across his back as he walked. Still, his voice had a rhythmic gait all its own, and he knew a thousand tales. He told of four gallant sisters who went out into the world and took up work as men. He told of a pig who grew wings of parchment and soared through the sky. He told of a man who hooked a monster that nearly dragged his boat undersea.

The forest loomed dark all around them. It rustled and

snapped and moaned. Ever Lyf strained to hear the sounds of pursuing hoofbeats.

And yet . . . *an adventure!* There were moments when Lyf felt freed of some heaviness, released from her old, narrow life and launched into something new. And through it all the calm, smiling voice in the darkness steadied her, helped her to blunt her fears.

In time they emerged from the forest and wended up rocky escarpments where the wind whipped the mist into tatters and the stars came glimmering out. When the first traces of dawn touched the eastern horizon, they were high in the mountains. Kymo helped her down from the mule and handed her a heavy iron pot, bidding her to fetch water from a stream down the hill.

"Mama forbids me to fetch water, except from the well," Lyf said. "I'm not strong enough to carry it uphill."

Kymo cocked an eyebrow, gave her a long, appraising look. "Well, no mind," he said at last. "Then fetch us some kindling for a fire."

Before Lyf could protest, he went off for the water himself. Mama didn't like Lyf fetching kindling, either. It meant going into the forest, where it was dark. It was perilous in the forest, in the dark. But now . . . she had been in the forest for the better part of this night.

She took a deep breath and headed down toward a copse of scrubby pines that huddled on the slope. It was not *too* dark within. Lyf hurriedly scrabbled together a heap of fallen branches and lugged them back to the camp. Kymo, she saw, had already fetched water and was cutting larger branches for a shelter. He favored her with a nod and a smile as she dropped the kindling. Then, hardly breaking the rhythm of his ax, Kymo said, "Fetch Grumble down to the stream, there's a good lass, for her throat'll be sore parched."

Lyf hesitated. Leading Grumble to the stream was not the same as fetching water in a heavy kettle. Still, it was a trek, down the scree-covered slope, through dark trees and underbrush, and she was weak and weary and her head ached from hunger. Mama would not have allowed it. But Mama was not here. Likely she had forgotten to tell Kymo about the fever. Perhaps he had not seen the vermilion mark on her cheek. It had paled as the fever had waned, and now it hardly showed.

I will tell him, Lyf thought: about the fever when I was little, about how frail I am. But something in the resolute set of Kymo's back stopped her.

The stream was not so very far. And she would have Grumble with her.

Lyf untethered the mule and tugged on her rope. Grumble grumbled, but did not budge. "Come along, Grumble. Come along." Grumble balked and strained backward. Lyf sighed, walked back to the mule. Carefully, she reached up and scratched in Grumble's left ear. Grumble shot forward; Lyf leapt aside and slipped on a patch of loose scree. Quickly she stood and, making for the stream, led the compliant mule down to drink.

She returned more tired than ever, and yet feeling somehow stronger than before. Mama would have been surprised to see what she had done. Kymo scooped her out a bowl of oat porridge, then lowered himself stiffly to sit on a rock. Lyf joined him, watched the sunrise as she gulped down her portion. It was warm and spicy and satisfying. And when they were done, Kymo bade Lyf scrub their bowls with sand while he set out sleeping skins within the lean-to shelter he had made. Lyf lay down to rest then as Kymo took out his harp and told a tale about a beetle that soared above the sky and found another world, where giant beetles dwelt. It was a wondrous tale, and Lyf *did* want to hear the end of it. But her eyelids were heavy—her whole head felt heavy—and her mind drifted away from the words and into sleep.

She awoke past midday to the pittering of rain on the branches of the shelter. The sky was all-over gray, lending a dull, shadowless cast to the light.

Kymo was packing the mule. He turned round at the crunch of her boot on the scree. "We're all but ready now," he said. Tightening the cinch, he motioned her near and boosted her up onto Grumble. He handed her a loaf, some cheese, and a skin of weak brew, then went round to the fore. Lyf scratched; Grumble lurched. They were off.

The rain did not let up through all that dreary afternoon. It pricked hollowly on Lyf's hood as she rode; it beaded on the fabric of her cloak. The smell of wet wool filled her nose. As they moved to lower, forested ground, the rain grew louder, slapping hard against the trees. Before long, the wet soaked clear through Lyf's cloak, to her kirtle, to her shift. The damp chill seeped down into her bones. She would catch her death, Mama would say if she knew. Still, the forest seemed less fearsome this day, which freed Lyf's mind to think. That message. What could it bode? She might take it from her sash and read it. But the rain would bleed the ink, would ruin it.

Something to do with Kaeldra. Something that others might try to pry out. Lyf's thoughts swirled with dark imaginings of pursuing Krags, of perils to Kaeldra . . . and to herself.

Green eyes, the soldier had said. Kaeldra's eyes were green—green-flecked, at any rate. And yet not nearly so green as Lyf's. "Mine are only inherited," Kaeldra had once told her, "but yours are undiluted by other bloodlines—straight from the dragon's milk."

Kaeldra was a Krag—tall and blond—not small and dark-haired like Lyf and most Elythians. They were not blood kin. Even so, Lyf and Kaeldra had been raised as sisters. Granmyr had taken in Kaeldra before Lyf was born. Not a popular thing to do, for Krags were despised hereabouts. They had invaded Elythia, occupying the castles and the most fertile land, seizing food and livestock whenever it suited them, elevating those who supported them to positions of power.

The Krags misliked all green-eyed ones—whether Kraggish or no—because of the power they held over dragons. Kaeldra's green-flecked eyes had been a danger to her even as a babe. Dragon-sayers' eyes, they called them.

"Lyf?" Kymo turned around to look at her. "I'm in a mind to tell a story. Do you fancy hearing one?"

"Yes," Lyf began, and then amended, "Well, no. First I would like to know . . . have you seen this place where Kaeldra lives? Do they keep the draclings there?"

Kymo laughed. "Yes, I've seen it, and no, the draclings aren't there. Jeorg and Kaeldra go to the dragons when they are needed—many dragon caves, scattered near and far."

"Have you ever seen a dracling?"

"No," Kymo said, "though I hope I will one day."

Lyf secretly hoped to see one also. Long had she heard talk of draclings—ever since Kaeldra had gone to fetch dragon's milk. There had been three draclings then, and Kaeldra had come to love them. She had taken them away when their lives were imperiled.

And now there were other clutches, other draclings—all imperiled. Men had always hunted dragons, but never so relentlessly as in this past year. Kaeldra had feared that soldiers would one day come for her, demanding that she track down dragons to kill. So she and Jeorg had fled into hiding with their green-eyed son, Owyn. Still, Kaeldra would not abandon her cause—to keep the draclings safe until they could fly to the far northern land where the rest of their kyn dwelt. Though how she did so, Lyf did not know.

Now Kymo began with a tale, and Lyf gratefully turned her mind from her own worries to the troubles of others. He told of a girl who found an enchanted box and cast a spell that went awry; of a lizard who befriended a child who had fallen from the stars; of a fool who sought a magical leaf that would make him disappear. Kymo told as well of his hopes to find a wife—a comely lass and clever, but above all, one well-skilled with the stew pot. And yet there were times in their journey when all was silent, save for the patter of rain, the dripping of water from the trees, and the tread of Kymo's and Grumble's footfalls on the sodden track. Often it seemed that they did not move at all, but only trod in one place as the trees moved ever toward them, growing darker and darker as they neared and then fading in the distance behind.

It was late in the day when they turned off onto a muddy path. Lyf shivered constantly now, and her teeth had begun to chatter.

Before long the path ended in a tangle of parsebramble and wild nectarvine. Kymo drew on a pair of heavy, gauntleted gloves and began tugging at the snarl. To Lyf's astonishment, it moved easily aside; and yet more brambles lay behind it. Kymo turned back to her and smiled. "A gate," he said.

"We're nearly there?"

"Nearly." Kymo dragged aside an especially unwieldy mass of brambles, and then another and another, opening up a corridor just wide enough for Grumble. Lyf scratched; Grumble lurched forward. There came a rustling of brambles as Kymo closed the gap behind. A soft luminescence filtered through the trees ahead.

A clearing?

Yes, a clearing.

They emerged from the wood, and Lyf saw just ahead a crumbling stone wall with an iron-barred gate. And beyond . . . she strained to make it out through the rain and swirling fog.

It was a ruin. It loomed like a broken-backed giant: cottage and byre and shed all run together in a single, long structure. The slate roof had collapsed in one place; the windows looked out with dark, blank eyes. It was still—utterly still—save for a thin, blue twist of woodsmoke that wound up into the sky.

"Jeorg?" Kymo called. "Kaeldra?"

"Is this . . . where they live?" Lyf asked, gazing at the ferns sprouting from the roof, the shutters dangling from the windows.

Kymo nodded. "They're here, never doubt—"

A twig snapped behind them. Lyf twisted round to see an archer, a bearded archer.

His crossbow was drawn taut, the bolt aimed straight at her.

Harper's Tale

Why, you ask, my lord, would a man be a friend to dragons? Or a woman, for that matter? For many of the dragons' friends were women.

All had their reasons.

Some were more foes to the Krags than friends to dragons. Though the Krags had long ago subdued Elythia, some (though not myself, my lords—I wouldn't dream it!) wished to push them out. Or, failing that, to thwart them however they might. These folk did not split hairs between the queen's soldiers and those loyal to her cousin, the king. *Any* Kragish army invulnerable to the sword was greatly to be dreaded.

And others . . .

Have you ever seen a dragon soaring on the wind, my ladies?

No? I guessed not. You're all of you far too young.

Some deem my arts great (though I am no proper judge of it)—but even I cannot school you in the wonder of dragons.

Would you slay all the eagles as a pestilence? Would you outlaw the thunder for its din?

If you had never known them, you wouldn't mourn their loss. But if you had known them . . . the world would ever have a great, gaping hole in it, where splendor once had dwelt.

For whatever motives, my lords and ladies, the friends of dragons conspired.

Chapter 4

Auntie Lyf

Lyf stared at the archer and could not move. His features were veiled by the dark, streaking rain, but he loomed above Kymo, and his beard bristled full and blond.

A Krag, he was.

Kymo stepped toward him. "Jeorg?" he said.

Jeorg? But Jeorg had no beard. . . .

The archer lowered his bow. "Kymo, is it? And . . . will that be Lyf?"

It *was* Jeorg—she knew him by his voice.

He shouldered his bow and ran then. He lifted her off of Grumble and hugged her tight. "Lyfling!" he said.

"Jeorg . . . you grew a beard!"

"Does it please you?"

Lyf hesitated. "I don't know. It makes you . . . strange."

Jeorg laughed, setting her on the ground, and then his

face grew grave. "What brings you here?"—he turned to Kymo—"and you? Has ill befallen any at home—the girls? Granmyr?"

"No. They're well. But the queen's men came seeking Kaeldra—or, failing her, *this* green-eyed one. And so Granmyr thought it safer to send her to you."

"And glad I am that she has," Jeorg said, turning to Lyf, "and Kaeldra will be gladder still." He cupped his hands to his mouth. "Kaeldra!" he bellowed. "It is Lyf! *Lyf!*"

Down near the ruin Lyf could see movement: someone coming, someone running. *Kaeldra.* Lyf sprinted to the gate, grabbed the rusty iron bars and peered between them. Yes, Kaeldra—and two others coming behind: a thin, hawk-nosed man and a stocky little boy. The man would be Nysien, Mirym's husband; the boy would be Owyn, Jeorg and Kaeldra's youngest. Now Kaeldra was grating back the heavy bolt; she enfolded Lyf in her arms. Lyf felt a wave of comfort such as she had not known since she had left home. Kaeldra would take care of her. She had done so before—she had saved her life—and now she would again.

"Are you well? Are all well at home?" Kaeldra asked at last. "Our girls? Granmyr? Mirym? Your mother?"

"Granmyr and Mama are well. And Mirym too, though she pines for Nysien. And Lyska and Aryanna—I saw them, not a half-moon since. They are well, but they miss you."

Kaeldra nodded. "This will all be over soon, and then we will be"—her voice caught; she swallowed—"together."

Kaeldra sorely yearned for her daughters—that was plain to see. She and Jeorg had not brought them here because there was no one to care for them when she journeyed off to do her work with dragons. Neither was it safe for them in

Granmyr's home. Though the girls' eyes were blue, they still were Kaeldra's daughters, and so at risk. She had left them in care of a friend some way from home.

With Owyn there had been no choice. He had his mother's eyes—brightly flecked with green. The friend who kept the girls would not take him for fear his dragon-sayer's eyes would put her in peril as well.

So Kaeldra had brought him here. She had begged to bring Lyf, but Mama would not hear of it. Not until now.

"Why," Kaeldra asked, "come you *now?*"

"The queen's men came seeking you—and me because of my eyes."

"Oh, Lyfling." Kaeldra pulled Lyf to her again, and Lyf smelled the familiar smell of her, felt the warm softness of her as Kaeldra stroked her hair. But her belly... it felt hard....

Lyf pulled away. "Are you...?"

Kaeldra smiled and laid both hands flat on her belly. "Three moon-turns now," she said. "A late-harvest child, 'twill be."

A sudden loud clanking assailed them; Lyf whirled round to see Owyn beating a metal cup with a spoon. "I beat the drums!" he said in a voice startlingly husky for such a youngling. "Boom! Boom! I beat them!"

"Owyn!" Kaeldra said. "Hush, now!" Gently stripping him of cup and spoon, she took his hand. "This is your Auntie Lyf. You recall your Auntie Lyf!"

"Why?" Owyn asked. He peered up at her from beneath his thatch of red-gold hair. His face was so begrimed, Lyf could barely make out the freckles that sprinkled his snubby nose. "I beat the drums!" he mumbled, then he spun round and chugged away. It pained Lyf that he did not seem to remember her. A year it had been since they had left. The child had grown; ever he was growing. Three winters now he had. He stood sturdily on his feet, seeming a full head taller than when last she had seen him.

Kaeldra sighed. "My little drummer boy. He will warm to you soon enough. But now—*you* are the one who needs warming. You're soaked clear to the skin." She took Lyf's arm and led her through the gateway, leaving the men to stable Grumble.

It was, Lyf thought as they approached the ruin, even more dreary a place than it had seemed on first sight. Moss dripped from the broken-down roof, and black mold crept up the stones from the sodden ground. It was large—larger than any dwelling Lyf had seen—and yet much of it was crumbled and overgrown by a tangle of thorny bushes. Rosebushes, Lyf guessed. She was surprised that Kaeldra would let them go untended; she took such pains with her roses at home.

But when she stepped over the threshold, Lyf stared in wonderment. The floor was newly swept and strewn with clean rushes. Herbs hung in fragrant bunches from the rafters above Kaeldra's claywheel. The walls, though blackened with smoke, were sound—as was the roof. A fire crackled in a makeshift hearth in the middle of the floor, and savory smells arose from a stew pot.

"What sort of . . . cottage is this?" Lyf asked. "Is it from the olden times, the time of the road builders?"

"Yes. We thought it best to keep the fallen-down parts fallen-down, so that none may guess we are here. But my fingers itch to tend the roses. Jeorg won't allow it. He frets even about the smoke—but we must have fire."

"Do you still . . . work the clay?" Kaeldra could see things in the spinning clay. Things that had happened in the past, or very far away.

Kaeldra sighed. "Not often. It is not as it was. Does Granmyr still work it?"

"Sometimes. But she says the same, that the visions grow faint. Or refuse to come at all."

Shaking her head, Kaeldra thrust a kirtle and shift into Lyf's arms. "Well, then, let's get you dry. These are mine, and so they will be large for you. But they're not soaking wet, at any pass."

Lyf peeled off her drenched garb and draped it over a bench by the fire. She slipped gratefully into the dry garments Kaeldra had given her. They were drab-hued and cut long—unlike the bright, shorter gowns Kaeldra had worn at home. The kirtle's sleeves hung well below Lyf's hands, and its hem dragged upon the floor.

Kaeldra laughed softly when Lyf was done. "You look to be garbed in giant's dress—and so you are, I suppose. I have ever felt like a giantess among you Elythians." She rolled up Lyf's sleeves, then moved away past the claywheel to a chest behind a door. Drawing out a long, gray-blue sash, she fastened it about Lyf and bloused up the kirtle so that it came up off the floor.

The sash.

"Wait, there's something I must show you." Lyf rummaged through her wet clothes. There. The message. Explaining how she had come by it, she handed it to Kaeldra.

Kaeldra eyed Lyf sharply before taking it; she knew that Lyf was forbidden to ken with birds. Then she bore the message to the fire and labored to read it.

Lyf studied Kaeldra's face in the firelight. There were furrows in her brow and at the edges of her mouth that Lyf did not recall having seen before. Her straw-colored hair seemed limp and had lost its luster. Tired she looked—and also sad. As Lyf watched, alarm swept across Kaeldra's face. "Jeorg!" Kaeldra called, then moved to the door and flung it wide. "Jeorg!"

He came running from the courtyard, with Nysien and Kymo behind.

"The mother is slain," Kaeldra said.

Jeorg looked at her blankly.

"The dragon, the one we fetched the orphaned draclings to. She is slain."

"What!" Jeorg snatched the message from Kaeldra's outstretched hand and went to the fire, reading it by the flame. He uttered a curse.

"We must fetch the draclings," he said. "At once."

It was *not* at once, as it happened, for there was much to attend to, and most of it had to do with Owyn and Lyf. The children must stay, Kaeldra said. The journey was too perilous, and Lyf was already too far spent. But Kaeldra *must* go, it seemed, and Jeorg would not allow it without his protection, and Nysien, who might have helped, insisted on going elsewhere to muster a troop of archers. "There are many who are loyal to me," he said, "and I know they will rally round."

"We don't need a troop of archers," Jeorg said, visibly irked. "We have done this many times before. If you would wait here, with the children—"

"I? With the children?" Nysien raised a thin, dark brow, incredulous. And it was unthinkable to Lyf that he would tend to her and Owyn. He was of noble blood, and ever mindful of it. He even looked noble—tall, for an Elythian, and lean, with slender hands and a curving, princely nose.

And yet the Krags had seized all his lands; he was penniless.

There were many who had marveled when Nysien had taken Mirym as his bride. Why would he lower himself to marry a common lass—even one of uncommon beauty?

But the marvelers had not seen Nysien as Lyf had—weak and raving with wound fever, fleeing the Krags. He had led a troop of archers to win back his lands—and failed. When he blundered, half-dead, into the Elythian hills, Granmyr took him in and nursed him back to health. Lyf had marked how Mirym looked at him, how in time he had returned her looks. He had made promises to her when ill that he was bound to keep when well.

Yet Nysien had grown ever more restless on the farm. He seethed with a consuming hatred of the Krags and with schemes to recover his lost lands. He had pressed Kaeldra and Jeorg to let him help with the draclings—more, Lyf suspected, for vengeance on the Krags than for love of dragon kyn.

Now Kymo broke in placatingly, and the disputation went round and round. Lyf sat huddled by the fire, weary to the bone and yet anxious to hear all—for her fate hinged on what came of this colloquy.

The mother they spoke of, it seemed, was a dragon—the last but one of the mother dragons left in this land. An old friend of Kaeldra's had sent the message telling of the dragon's death.

"He writes that a troop of Kragish soldiers came through his steading, pillaging for food," Kaeldra said. "They had killed the dragon, had cut out her heart, and were fetching it to the queen. But they couldn't find the draclings and had given up the search. They had already sent three of their number searching for *me* to find the draclings." She paused, thinking. "Those must have been the soldiers at Granmyr's cottage."

"We had given that dragon three orphaned clutches to care for," Jeorg told Kymo. "*Three.*"

"And now the draclings are alone," Kaeldra said, "with none to feed them, and none to shield them from harm."

"If they're yet alive." Jeorg was grim.

Kaeldra looked at the message again. "It says the mother was slain well away from any cave, so there's hope we may yet find them and take them north to the last remaining dragon dam. But the children . . ." She cast a glance at Lyf and Owyn.

Nysien looked impatient. "Leave them stay with the woman you left Owyn with before."

"She took the lung fever over the winter and died," Kaeldra said. "I have told you this. If you had fetched the help you promised, those who are loyal to you—"

"I *will* fetch them! Give me time!"

"—then we could have all of our children here with us—not scattered throughout Elythia."

"I could spare a day or two to take the younglings home," Kymo offered.

"They can't return home," Kaeldra said. "It's too perilous there."

"Well, is there another place? Are any of the dove sign nearby?"

"None near *enough*."

"It seems nothing will please you in this," Nysien said.

"I need to know the younglings are safe! I . . ."

There was a tugging at Lyf's kirtle. Lyf glanced down to

see Owyn looking up at her. "Egg," he said. "I will show you the egg." He yanked at the end of her sash.

"No, not now," Lyf said softly. "I need to hear—"

Owyn's face crumpled. He let out a hoarse, piercing wail, then pounded away on chunky legs.

Kaeldra sighed and started toward him. "Oh, Owyn . . ."

"Let Lyf make herself of use," Nysien said. "We need to settle this now."

Kaeldra looked uncertain. Behind her, Kymo mouthed at Lyf, "Go."

Lyf turned and followed after Owyn. Soon enough she would find out whether she was to leave or stay.

Owyn forgave her on the instant, scrubbing the tears from his eyes with grimy fists. He tugged her through a room with straw pallets laid out on the floor, and through a storeroom jammed with sacks and crates and bales. Then out a back doorway they went, skirting the wreck of a room where the roof had caved in.

A cooing sound: Owyn led her past a brambly hedge to a round stone building with a conical slate roof. The dovecote. Lyf halted, knowing she should not go within. But when Owyn tugged at her sash and she still did not budge, his lower lip started to quiver. Well, she did not *have* to ken with them if she did not wish it; she would take care.

"Fetch the egg," Owyn said, taking hold of her sash and hauling her within.

The rich, musty smell of feathers and sawdust and guano engulfed Lyf as she entered. She could hear flutterings and the scratching of bird claws on stone, all overlaid with the deep, contented burblings of doves on the nest. The soft gray light of dusk, spilling down from an opening in the roof, illumined the stone crannies that encircled her. Deeply shadowed, the birds in their niches turned their red-rimmed eyes to stare.

Owyn pulled on Lyf's hand and pointed up. "Fetch the egg."

It lay upon the stone nesting wall, just below the cone of the roof. It must not truly be an egg, Lyf thought. No egg could be that large. Whatever it was, it seemed to catch all the light of that place and hold it within.

A ladder lay against the wall, but still Lyf hesitated. Whatever sort of bird might have laid that egg... she could not imagine. Perhaps it was an alabaster stone....

Then all at once Lyf *knew* what manner of egg it was.

A dragon egg.

Lyf sucked in her breath and stepped back. "No," she said to Owyn, "I will not fetch it. It—"

Owyn's lower lip quivered again. His face reddened; tears spilled over the rims of his eyes. "Why?" he asked. His husky voice cracked and rose shrilly. "Fetch the egg!"

Lyf huffed out a sigh, eyeing Owyn and then the egg. Well, what harm to humor him? Besides, she had never seen a dragon egg, and this ... she wanted to see it better.

"Very well!" Lyf said and, taking the ladder, moved it to just below the egg. "See? I'm fetching it! Don't cry!"

Carefully she scaled the ladder. Below, the crying abruptly ceased, replaced by loud, wet sniffles. When Lyf reached the egg, she stopped. It was as large as her own head, she guessed, and gray-white, tinged with green. The shell was not perfectly smooth. There were grooves on it, thin grooves that formed boxy figures, like the patterns on a tortoise's shell. Lyf touched the egg, then gingerly picked it up. It was heavy, but neither hard nor brittle; it gave a little to her touch. An odd, low vibration trembled against her fingers.

"Fetch the egg!"

Cradling the egg against her side, Lyf backed down the ladder.

She scraped together a heap of wood shavings with her feet, then settled the egg therein. Owyn squatted down beside it, moving his hands over its surface. He closed his eyes and began to hum.

Lyf's hands moved to touch the egg. The vibration passed through her fingertips and tingled in her palms. It almost seemed to . . . *hum.* Yes, it did—but faintly, and only when she touched it. It was a comforting sound—a sound, she thought, she could listen to forever.

"Lyf?"

Lyf leapt guiltily to her feet. Kaeldra stood in the doorway.

"I'm sorry; Owyn brought me here; I—"

Kaeldra waved aside her apology. "Well, and what do you make of our egg?"

"It is . . . a dragon egg?"

Kaeldra nodded. "I found it behind a rock in a cave where the other eggs had been broken and licked clean. By wolves, most like. But they missed this one. Jeorg deemed it dead, but . . . I sensed something, a faint trembling . . ." She paused. "Do you sense it too?"

"Oh, yes!"

Kaeldra eyed her oddly, seemed to wait for more.

"A trembling and . . . it hums."

Kaeldra nodded, unsurprised. She moved to pick up the egg. "We're going now—you and Owyn will come with us—and we need to take this, too." She paused, took thought. "Would *you* like to tend to the egg?"

"Yes!" Lyf said. "Oh, yes!"

Harper's Tale

The dragon friends were scattered throughout the land. Most knew only one or two or three of the others. It was not a thing you would boast of. It was perilous to own. And yet there was a sign, a secret sign, by which one dragon friend might be known to another. It might be carved upon a lintel, or drawn with a toe in the dirt, or worn as an amulet round the neck.

The sign of the dove.

Why *dove* you ask, my lord?

Be still and I will tell you!

Chief among the dragon friends were Kaeldra Dragon-sayer and her husband, Jeorg. They crossed the land provisioning the friends with banded message birds. Seabirds they were at first, but Jeorg soon found doves more suited to the work. If a friend heard of a dragon hatching, or a dragon slaying, or a dragon sighting, he would ink the dove's band with his mark. Or, if he were schooled in letters, he would tie a message to the bird's foot. Jeorg had trained the doves to return to a cottage in the hills of Elythia, where Kaeldra's Granmyr lived. And she would convey the message to Kaeldra.

And what of Lyf, you ask?

Would you fetch me a cup of brew, my lass? This tale telling is thirsty work.

So: What of Lyf?

Patience, my lady. I come to her anon.

Chapter 5

Dragon's Cave

Lyf curled up on a straw pallet with Owyn and the egg while the preparations for leaving went on all around them. Owyn snuggled close; before long Lyf could feel the slow, soft rise and fall of his breath. Sleep washed over her in a wave.

Then Kaeldra was shaking her, rousing her. Lyf slipped into her shift and kirtle, which were all but dry. Her cloak was still damp. Kaeldra lent her one, which fit long but did not drag on the ground. Then Kaeldra showed her a carrier she had devised: a grain sack rigged with a strap to loop around Lyf's neck.

"Wear it thus, to carry the egg in front," Kaeldra said, drawing the loop over Lyf's head. Kaeldra picked up the egg and gently slipped it inside. It felt heavy, but secure. Lyf splayed her hands across it to feel it, to support it, then laughed at herself.

"It must look as if I am with child," she said. "Or—with dragon."

Kaeldra smiled wanly. She picked up her sleeping son, then made for the courtyard, shooing Lyf before.

It was well past midnight—and dark. Few stars shone in the sky, and a fine, chill drizzle sifted down. Jeorg helped Lyf climb astride his great piebald stallion, then mounted up behind her. Owyn, his face sleepy and slack, rode with Kaeldra. Kymo came last, riding one of Jeorg's horses and leading Grumble behind. Lyf did not see Nysien; she guessed he had already left in search of archers.

At first Lyf clutched the piebald's mane with both hands and hugged its back close with her knees. But they moved at a plodding pace, and Jeorg kept one arm about her; there was little danger she would fall. Lyf's eyelids grew heavy; she leaned back against Jeorg and gave herself to the horse's swaying motion. One hand strayed to touch the egg within its sack; its vibration lulled her. She slept.

And yet it was a fitful sleep, broken by clatterings of hooves on rock, of branches whipping at her face, of sudden lurches as the horse broke its stride on some steep stretch of path. Once, the piebald got a rock wedged in its hoof; Jeorg had to dismount and pry it out. Another time, Kaeldra discovered that the marking sack was empty. Mounted on Kymo's mule, it had leaked out a thin stream of yellow sand to show Nysien the way. All waited, watching the dawn bloom up between the trees, as Jeorg switched sacks and cut another hole.

Lyf drowsed again, but after a time was awakened by droning voices. "Still, when the draclings hatched, what did the three of you do to help?" Kymo was saying. "I thought you must have a fighting force to keep the queen's men at bay.

But only three—not counting the mighty Owyn, of course. But nonetheless. You're greatly outnumbered."

Lyf, pretending to sleep, listened hard. She, too, had wondered about this. But whenever she had asked, her elders had made shift to speak of other matters.

"True"—the voice was Kaeldra's—"*if* the soldiers discovered the dragons' presence. But if we could beg or steal enough meat to keep the mother dragon fed and well in milk until the draclings were old enough to fly, the soldiers might never find them. Or so we hoped. Where we could come by fish, our task was the easier. With a full belly, a dragon need not raid, and few folk would learn of its presence. And many who did know were content to turn a blind eye."

"In this," Jeorg said, "we're aided by the queen, if she but knew it. The farmers would as lief thwart Kragish royalty as not—and the price of a lamb or two is none too great."

"So then, how many clutches have you saved?" Kymo asked.

"Seven." Kaeldra's voice again. "But only two of the mothers have left this land alive. The rest have been killed—though we found their clutches and took them to stay with other dragon dams. This last one who was killed had the care of three new clutches, and her own as well. Now there's only one mother left, and she's in a cave far to the north. If we can't find the missing draclings and fetch them to her before she flies. . . ." Her voice trailed off.

"Couldn't you call the grown dragons from the place where they live to come fetch the draclings? You did that once, I know."

"Don't you think I've tried?" Kaeldra sounded angry. "But they won't come to me anymore. It was just the once they came, and that time they were tricked! I fear they don't trust me. Or maybe. . . . I can't *bear* them the way I used to—even the little ones, even when they're right before me. Maybe I'm growing deaf to them, and they to me. Or maybe. . . Even my clay workings have failed me. And Granmyr's clay workings . . . they're weaker too. All magic is weaker, save for some of the herbal arts.

"It's as if magic is leaching out of this land as the Ancient Ones take leave of it. As if there can be no enchantments without dragons."

No one spoke for a moment, and Lyf thought they were done. But then she heard Jeorg's voice, coming in low: "It's the cogging bounty hunters that vex me most. Elythians they are—selling out to the Kragish queen for gold. And if"—his voice grew quieter still—"they believe a green-eyed child can help them find a dragon, they will not balk at taking her—or him."

"I fear the queen's soldiers most," Kaeldra said. "They may have tone pipes—though I hope not. Most no longer believe in the pipes' hold over dragons."

Kaeldra had spoken of these before: silver pipes whose tones could entrance a score of dragons. She had thwarted the pipes once, though Lyf did not know how.

"And do you believe in, then, this thing the queen claims," Kymo asked, "that if a man eats a dragon's heart, he is proof against sharp metal?"

Jeorg said nothing then, but Lyf felt him shift behind her. The sounds of the other horses grew fainter. Lyf peered out and saw that the trail had narrowed. Kaeldra murmured something that Lyf could not hear, and Kymo answered back, but they were well behind now and muffled by the thud of the piebald's hooves.

The shadows had grown long when they came to a halt. It was a high, rocky place where they had come. Clouds roiled above, bluish gray and sullen. The trees—what few there were—stood bent and hunched, cringing away from the wind. Jeorg dismounted and Lyf made to come down after, but he put out a hand to stop her. "Stay for now," he said. "Kaeldra and I are going ahead to the cave. Wait here with Kymo."

Kaeldra, Lyf saw, had also lit down and was handing over Owyn to Kymo. "I beat the drums," Owyn said.

Kaeldra kissed a finger, then laid it to Owyn's cheek. To Kymo, she said, "Stay well back from us when we come down with the draclings. They'll do you no harm, but the horses may well be affrighted."

"What will you do with them?" Lyf asked.

"Jeorg and I will herd them before us. You follow until we reach Yanil's farm, just east of these mountains. There's a dove sign carved on his lintel." Kaeldra smiled reassuringly at Lyf. "You've heard me tell of my friend Yanil. And he's the one who sent the message telling of the dragon's death. He'll fold you and Owyn in with his own brood until Jeorg and I return. I trust him completely—and so must you."

"Where will *you* go?"

"The last dragon mother lairs far to the north, where the land meets the Northern Sea. Jeorg and I will take the draclings to her. They'll fly with her to their land across the waters."

Lyf gripped Kaeldra's arm. "I'm afraid," she said.

Kaeldra slipped a hand over Lyf's. "No need to fear," she said. "Only stay back! And mind you—don't try to ken with them. Do you promise?"

Lyf nodded.

Jeorg drew a bolt from his quiver; they headed uphill. Lyf

hugged the egg against herself. The hum coursed through her body but did not settle her mind. To see a dracling—at last. Lyf did not know whether she was more eager or more afraid. "Where is the cave?" she asked Kymo. "I can't see it."

He pointed to a shadow in the craggy tor ahead.

Silently they watched as Kaeldra and Jeorg wended up the rocky track. "Mama," Owyn said hoarsely. "Mama."

Kymo jostled him gently. "Did ever I tell the tale of your namesake, Owyn of—"

Owyn thrashed his arms; his face turned red. *"Mama!"* he wailed.

As they watched, Kaeldra and Jeorg disappeared into the shadow.

An eagle soared into view and circled overhead. Jeorg's horse snorted and twitched. Owyn calmed at last to a strip of salted meat and a tale of a changeling imp. But Lyf kept her gaze fixed upon the shadow where Kaeldra and Jeorg had vanished. Still no sight of them.

Then at once—a movement. Jeorg. He was coming down the slope. He moved his arms in a gesture none could mistake: *Come!*

They made their way up to the cave more slowly on horseback than Kaeldra and Jeorg had gone afoot. Lyf went before, wary of controlling Jeorg's massive horse, so much higher off the ground than the shaggy little ponies she was wont to ride. The piebald stumbled on loose scree, sending down clattering rivulets of rock. Approaching the cave, it began to snort and balk. *It smells dragon*, Lyf thought—and a shiver ran down her spine.

The cave was immense, angling up above them like the sky on a starless night. Two candles burned some way within, and there Lyf made out Kaeldra and Jeorg. She looked about for draclings, but saw none. And yet there was a smell—a strange, scorched smell.

"Where could they have *gone?*" Kaeldra's anguish echoed and reechoed, seeming to swell and fill the cavern.

Gone?

Jeorg's voice rumbled low and indistinct. "Can't be far," Lyf thought she heard him say.

So the draclings were not here. Lyf felt a flicker of disappointment.

Kymo helped her dismount; she took care not to squash the egg. She tethered the horse to an outcropping of rock, then drew near to Kaeldra and Jeorg. They were arguing—not in anger at each other, but in vexation at the pass they had come to, and in disagreement on where to go next.

". . . must divide up and go *now,*" Kaeldra was saying, "and catch them before nightfall. No telling what may befall them—"

"I *will* not leave you," Jeorg said. "We must stop and take thought—or end up worse than we are now. First we look for tracks—"

"Tracks! In rock?"

"—and if we find none, we will put our heads together, consider carefully where they are most like to have gone."

"Too slow! They're fleeing as we speak! We must—"

Now Kymo joined in the contention as well, ignoring Owyn, ignoring Lyf.

"Boom! I beat the drums!"

Lyf turned to see Owyn pounding on a boulder with two sticks. He pounded again, then turned and made for the dark inner recesses of the cave.

"Owyn, no!" Kaeldra said, then cast Lyf a pleading look and held out her candle to her.

Lyf sighed and took the candle. Kaeldra plucked at her sleeve, mouthed *Thank you,* then turned back to Jeorg and Kymo.

Lyf caught up to Owyn a little way back in the cave. She considered picking him up and fetching him back to the others—but the egg would get in the way and, in any case, Owyn would likely work himself into a pother. He was well content for now to beat his fanciful drumsticks on fanciful drums. No harm in that.

The cave narrowed as they went. Candlelight spilled on the ground before Lyf's feet; she picked her way through the tumble of rocks. Once, she nearly stumbled on a heap of bones. She shivered.

Dragon's prey.

Owyn stumped into every cranny and cavelet he encountered, beating on the cave walls all the while. It grew colder, damper, darker. Lyf had just decided to brave Owyn's fury and fetch him back to the others when all at once there came a great echoing shout. She turned, stared back at the cave mouth. Dark shadows swarmed into the light. Men! Many men. Nysien's archers?

They surged into the cavern, still shouting. Lyf heard Kaeldra scream; then her voice suddenly ceased, as if cut off.

Lyf started forward, stopped, stood frozen, her heart in her mouth. Kaeldra.... On impulse, Lyf blew out her candle.

What had befallen? Should she go to see? Or ...

The voices swelled in contention. Then ...

"Lyf! Owyn!" It was an Elythian voice, though one she did not know. A flickering yellow glow bobbed slowly toward her.

Lyf hesitated. If it had been Kaeldra who had called, she would have gone to her, no question. But a stranger . . .

He called again. All other voices were still. And now, in the light of the approaching candle, Lyf could make out a dark form.

"No!" Kaeldra's voice rang out suddenly, and at the same time there was a sharp, guttural curse.

Scuffling noises. A muffled scream.

What had she meant by *No*?

Was she hurt?

Was it a warning?

Lyf waited as long as she could bear it, but the candle bobbed ever nearer, and soon she would have no choice. Then at once her feet whirled round of their own accord and raced for the back of the cave.

Where was Owyn? She had forgotten about Owyn!

Black. All was black. She stumbled on a pile of rocks, caught herself, slowed to a walk. The egg. Mustn't break the egg. "Owyn," she whispered. "Owyn, where are you? Speak softly now—don't shout."

"Why?" came a soft, hoarse voice.

It was startlingly near. Lyf moved blindly toward the voice, scrabbling with her hands along the clammy cave walls. There. A niche—but too small for even Owyn. Now another—down low.

"Owyn," she breathed, "are you there?"

"Why?"

"Sh!"

Plague him with his *whys!* He was *ever* asking why, even when it made no sense. Sometimes, Lyf thought he just wanted to keep her talking.

She tried to crawl through the opening, but got stuck and

could go no farther. The egg. Must take off the egg. She hauled it up out of its carrier, set it down on the ground, and gently rolled it through. Then she crept through herself, thankful for once that she was small. Her head bumped something soft: Owyn. She groped one hand up his face, clamped it over his mouth, then brought her lips to his ear.

"Sh," she whispered. "We're playing a trick on the others."

Owyn pulled her hand away from his mouth. "But Mama—"

"She's playing too. Sh!"

Lyf scooted Owyn away from the opening and pulled him down onto her lap. She wrested the sticks from his hands and put a finger to his lips, wishing that she could go down inside him and silence him as she had the bird.

"Lyf?" came the man's voice. "Owyn?"

Owyn shook with held-in laughter. Lyf clasped her hand over his mouth.

"Come out now; don't be afeared. Kaeldra sent me to fetch you." The voice, full of false heartiness, echoed in the darkness.

Lyf could hear footsteps now, crunching on the rocks. More than one pair, it seemed to her. Then, "They're not here," came the voice. "Kaeldra claims they left them at a farm."

"You credit what *she* says?" Another voice—older, deeper, but still Elythian.

"Well, what of the draclings? He said there would be draclings."

"They were here. I can *smell* them."

"We should have followed longer, like Nysien told us. Till we were sure they had the draclings. We'd have got the wolf's head for Kaeldra *and* the beasts."

Lyf started. *Nysien?*

"Or *lost* both," the older-sounding man said.

"Lyf!" the other shouted. He was walking now, coming nearer. "Owyn! Come on, now! I've an apple for you."

Lyf squeezed Owyn. "Be still," she breathed.

But her mind was working fast, groping to understand. *Nysien had sent them?*

"They're not here," the younger one said at last. "Nysien said the girl is a cosseted milk coddle. She'd have run sniveling to her sister by now."

"I marked a light. They're here—but farther back!"

"You're the only one who saw. Likely your eyes played you a trick, getting used to the dark."

"My eyes see as well as yours!" Then, shouting, "Lyf! Owyn! Come out now or I'll flay you and string you up!"

Lyf hugged Owyn tightly to comfort him, to comfort *herself*. The men were close now, so close. Light seeped across the floor, flooding the tiny chamber where they hid. Lyf's bloodbeat pounded in her ears. Owyn wiggled to escape her restraining arms; she leaned in close and breathed, "Be still!" in his ear.

"Oh, that was clever of you," the younger one said. "Even if they *were* here, they'd never come out now."

"Well," the other growled, "I'll send a man back to the farm where Kaeldra said they left them. If the brats aren't there . . ."

The light ebbed away from the opening; the voices grew rumbly and faint. Owyn squirmed to free himself, but Lyf clamped him tight against her.

"Hush," she whispered. "Hush."

Harper's Tale

Whenever a dove's message told that a dragon dam had been slain, Kaeldra and Jeorg journeyed to the lair to save the draclings. This time that I tell of, three others rode along as well: Owyn, their son; Lyf (I come to her at last); and a harper. Some say this harper was the finest in all of Elythia, my ladies. But I am no judge of that.

Then, all but the two younglings were captured.

I tell only what I know, my lords. Some harpers give you stale old tales, warmed over with a few poor leeks and turnips stirred in to make them seem fresh. But this tale I tell you tonight is true. I know whereof I speak.

I do not know directly what passed in the cave with Lyf and Owyn, so I cannot tell you of that.

Still, I do know this for a surety: Kaeldra and Jeorg and the finest harper west of the Kragish Sea were trussed up like guinea fowl and taken on horseback to a castle in the Elythian woods.

CHAPTER 6

Alone

Lyf eased her hold on Owyn when she heard the men leaving, and loosed it altogether when the retreating clatter of hooves grew too faint to hear.

"Mama," Owyn whimpered. "I want Mama."

"She'll soon return," Lyf said, and then another lie: "She said to wait here." Before he could protest, she hugged him close on her lap and told him, as best she could recall it, one of Kymo's tales: the adventures of a girl who lived in a chicken hut.

Owyn called for his mother a time or two after that, but each time Lyf hushed him and went on with the story, adding new dangers to distract him. Her pulse beat hard and fast in her throat, but she kept her voice carefully calm. At last Owyn leaned back against her, growing heavier and heavier in her lap. His body softened, his head lolled to one side, his breath-rise came measured and slow. Thank the heavens he had been weary, else he would not have been so easily placated, and would no doubt have raised a wail heard clear across the mountains.

She kept on with the story long past when she knew Owyn slept, for she knew that when she stopped, she would have to think.

She did not want to think.

And yet the thoughts *would* come—dark and fearsome—thronging into her mind and breaking the thread of the story. At last she gave up the telling, let the tale drift away. Still she did not move to go, for it felt safer here in the cool, close darkness of the cave. None could see them here. None could find them.

Kaeldra's scream echoed and reechoed in Lyf's mind, striking terror every time. But she had shouted, "No," soon after, and so could not have been badly hurt.

Could she?

Nysien had led the men here, that was clear. He wouldn't let them harm her. Or would he?

What had the one man said? *We should have followed longer, like Nysien told us. We'd have got the wolf's head for Kaeldra* and *the beasts*.

A wolf's head on Kaeldra? Lyf knew that the Kragish queen had put out a wolf's head on dragons.

But on *Kaeldra*?

She shivered, suddenly chilled.

What to do? Where to go now?

They could not return home; home was too far. And the ruin . . . that was not safe. Nysien might return there anytime. But that farmer . . . the one Kaeldra had told of. Yanil, was he called?

He lived, Kaeldra had said, to the east of the mountains. He had sent the message about the dragon's death, and there was a dove carved on the lintel of his door.

But the horses were gone; the two of them must travel afoot. And Owyn would be slow. And they had no fire tools, and they had no food, and Lyf was hungry even now. And the forest . . . it was perilous in the forest, with none to defend them from wolves or holt cats . . . or bounty hunters.

Lyf felt the tears stinging her eyes. They were lost. They would be killed if they left this cave and would starve if they stayed within it. She sniffled, wiped her nose on her sleeve.

Then the bounty hunter's words came back to her. *She'd have run sniveling to her sister,* he had said. *A cosseted milk coddle,* he had called her.

Lyf drew herself up, indignant. Well, she was *not.* She would make her way to this Yanil's farm, and bring Owyn and the egg in tow.

She had no other choice.

Owyn did not wake when Lyf lifted him off her lap and gently laid him on the ground. She groped about on hands and knees until she brushed against the egg. She held if for a moment in her lap, letting the vibration calm her, then groped about some more, pushing the egg before her, until she found the cleft she had come in by. She rolled the egg through.

"Owyn," she said, shaking him gently. "Time to go."

"Mama." His voice was husky with sleep.

"We're going to find your mama," Lyf said. "Scoot out through the hole now, there's a big boy."

"Why?" Owyn asked, but Lyf ignored the question and gently prodded him out. She crawled out behind him, found the egg, and slipped it back into the carrier.

Darkness clotted thick about where now they stood, but ahead Lyf could see light: the flush of sunset beyond the arch of the cave; the pale, pinkish glow just within. She blundered her way over the rocky ground, holding Owyn's hand. "Mama," he said eagerly. "Mama. Mama." Lyf felt a sharp pang of guilt.

When they neared the cave mouth, Lyf stopped, uneasy. Might the hunters have left someone without, to watch for her and Owyn? No, she thought, and yet . . .

"Stay here," she said softly to Owyn.

"I want Mama!"

"Sh! We'll find her soon, but you need to be still. We're playing a trick."

"Why?"

"Sh. You'll see."

In the dim, rosy light, Lyf could see that Owyn was not as pleased with this game as he had been before. His face clouded over; Lyf feared that he would scream. She forced herself to sound cheerful. "It'll be merry when your mama and da see how clever you are. Now wait here," she said, coaxing him to one side of the opening and settling him behind an outcropping of rocks. "I'll soon return."

Owyn looked uncertain. "Why?"

"Wait here," Lyf whispered, backing toward the cave mouth. "And don't beat the drums! Sh!"

She edged out cautiously, stooping low in the shadows behind a clump of boulders. The air smelled fresh and the ground was sodden. It must have rained. Lyf crept from boulder to boulder until she could see the winding track they had taken to the cave. She scanned the track in the gathering dusk.

Nothing. They were alone. All was still save for the wind, which rattled in the tree branches and gusted in her ears.

The hunters must have gone.

She returned to the cave and found Owyn rubbing one eye with a fist. "Let's go," she said with forced cheerfulness. "We're off to find your mama."

"Why?" he asked.

"Because we want to find her. Don't you?"

Owyn nodded, regarding her with trusting, eager eyes. Dirt streaked his face; his hair was matted on one side and stuck straight up in back. He would hate her when he found out, when it became clear that they would not soon see Kaeldra. But for now, this was all she could do.

Lyf had noticed a narrow path that wound up the tor to the east. She shooed Owyn up before her; he found a stick and began thumping on boulders and trees. "I beat the drums," he said. Lyf, thinking to keep him in good humor, found a stick for herself and thumped away beside him.

She felt uneasy about the noise, but . . . *The hunters are gone,* she told herself. *They would have seized us by now if they weren't.* And the thumping made her feel braver, somehow.

The path crested the tor and then dipped down into a hollow crowded with needlecone trees. It was darker here, but twilight trickled through the branches and showed a muddy footpath. Lyf did not know for certain whether it headed toward Yanil's farm. But it seemed so. Another hill loomed before them, though not so high as the tor they had just climbed. Perhaps they had crossed the highest mountains. Perhaps they had not far to go. Perhaps this very night she would find Yanil, would tell him what had befallen Kaeldra and Jeorg and Kymo. Then he would take care of all.

Lyf had heard of Yanil in the tales Kaeldra told. He had taken her in and fed her. Later, he had sealed the draclings into casks so that they could stow away on a ship.

The woods closed in around them. Through the lattice of branches, Lyf caught a glimpse of moon. It shed only meager light—a pearly luminescence that gathered high up in the trees—but it was enough to show the path. The wind picked up and seethed fitfully in the treetops, shaking loose droplets of trapped rainwater.

A damp chill settled about Lyf's shoulders. Her neck chafed, and her back ached from the weight of the egg. Owyn was taken with sudden bursts of energy when he would gallop ahead on the path, brandishing his stick and shouting "Boom! Boom! Boom!" Lyf jogged after, the egg thumping painfully against her stomach. Then, as suddenly as they had begun, Owyn's bursts of energy would fizzle. He would halt, throw himself to the ground, and refuse to budge. "When will we find Mama?" he would whine. "I want Mama."

Lyf carried him on one hip until her arm and shoulder began to ache and her hand would not grip and he slipped out again, ready to run. He was *solid*, surprisingly heavy for one so young. Once, Lyf let him climb up and ride on her back. But she could not lug him more than a few steps in this wise before her back began to pain her so fiercely that she couldn't abide it, and her knees grew so weak she feared that they would fold.

Owyn began to cough, lightly at first, and then, as the night wore on, in long, hacking spasms. He no longer galloped, but dragged along the path, whining that he was tired, that he was hungry, that he was cold, that his feet hurt, that he wanted his mother. Lyf felt like whining too. She might have done so if there were someone to whine *to*. If there were someone to take care of her. But as it was . . .

She was the only one who could take care.

They would not reach Yanil's farm this night—now that was certain. She must find a place for them to rest. And the ground was yet too sodden to lie on. She had no ax to make shelter—nor even a knife. To be cold and wet at once . . . Owyn's throat-ill would only grow worse.

Lyf was no longer sure which way they were headed. The light in the forest had faded until it was impossible to see the path except by the gap of moonlit sky between the trees. And while it had seemed at first to lead east, the path had wound around and intertwined with other paths and now it was so narrow that it might not be a path at all, but only a trampled track for animals.

Holt cats? Wolves?

She stopped, listened hard. Wind shivered in the tree boughs, loud as a rushing stream. Below, on the ground, there were soft rustlings and scattered ominous *snaps*.

In the gloom not far ahead Lyf made out the shape of a wide-forking tree—perhaps wide enough for her and Owyn to nest in. It would not keep them safe from holt cats, but it would hold the wolves at bay. At the very least, it would get them off the wet ground.

Lyf led Owyn to the foot of the tree. He shivered, hacked out a cough. "Sit here," she said. She took off the egg carrier, handed it to him. Maybe the egg would give him comfort. "Hold this. I'll soon return."

"Why?" Owyn croaked hoarsely. He slumped against the tree, hugging the egg.

Lyf kilted her skirts, looking up. She had climbed a tree but once or twice before—Mama would not permit it—but it did not look so very hard. She jammed one boot against the bole above a protruding knob and, holding on to a sturdy branch, hauled herself up to the fork. There. Space enough for Owyn to nestle in the crotch of the branches and lean back against the thicker one. She could lash him to the branch with her sash. Lyf looked up and saw another fork above. She climbed up to it; the bough swayed a bit, made a rustling in the leaves. It was narrow here. Scary. But safer and drier than the ground.

She climbed back down, calling out, "We'll rest here, Owyn. I'll boost you up and—" Reaching the ground, she turned to where he sat—and stopped. The egg lay against the tree bole.

But Owyn was gone.

"Owyn!" Lyf called. "Owyn!"

Rustlings. Somewhere in the distance a stream gurgled. But of Owyn, not a sound.

Lyf looked about her, fear clutching at her throat. She could not see far, for darkness lay thick among the trees, clotting to blackness not far beyond. The moon had disappeared behind a shred of cloud.

"Owyn!"

No answer.

Hastily, Lyf slipped on the egg carrier, then moved forward along the trampled way. Vines tore at her legs; a tree branch whipped across her face. It was *not* a footpath, she admitted to herself. It may well have begun so, but now it was only an animal track, and they were well and truly lost. She called again for Owyn, then stood listening. The plash of running water. And then . . . a hoarse little cough.

Owyn!

She felt her way down the track as quickly as she could. It seemed to end at the foot of an enormous, hollowed-out stump. This looked to have been lightning-struck, for at about the height of Lyf's head the tree had split off and fallen to the forest floor.

"Owyn?"

A soft rumbling emanated from the stump. A scorched smell mingled with the scents of rain and leaves and rotted wood. Smoke? Lyf warily eyed the stump. It was larger than any tree stump she had seen. It sprouted with ferns and moss and fungus. A rubble of boulders stood beside it. Above the tallest rock were light patches on the stump, where the bark was freshly scraped off. Or kicked off—by someone climbing in.

"Owyn, are you in there?"

Silence. And then . . . another cough.

"*Owyn!*"

Muttering under her breath, Lyf clambered up onto the boulders, leaned against the stump, and peered over its rim. Darkness pooled within, but she thought she caught a movement. The moon must have come out just then, for at once there was light inside the stump: a soft liquid glimmering all around, and sharp, pinpoint gleams.

Eyes. A score of them and more, glinting green.

Dragon eyes.

Harper's Tale

All the dreary trek to the castle, a puzzle gnawed at Kaeldra and Jeorg and the harper:

How had the hunters known where to find them?

The captives spoke of this softly when chance provided, when their captors could not hear. They listened well to the men's talk, hoping some passing remark would make all clear.

Just happenstance, you say, my lady? They had been seen by chance?

Perhaps.

And yet, other likelihoods came to mind—one more than the rest. But the captives, especially Kaeldra, were loathe to embrace it.

Nysien. Kaeldra's sister's husband. Only he had known where they were bound.

Still, when the castle loomed before them and the guards

were found to be Krags, they knew it could not have been he. Even more when they laid eyes on the Kragish queen.

Nysien was renowned for his hatred of the Krags. He would sooner die than collude with them.

Or so the captives thought.

Oh—easy to scoff, my lord! I'll wager that you—knowing only what they knew then—would have judged the same.

CHAPTER 7

Hungry!

A spurt of blue flame sliced through the darkness, blinding Lyf, filling her lungs with smoke. She stumbled back down the boulders, away from the stump—then she heard Owyn's voice within.

"I tricked you! Ha! I tricked you!"

Lyf stopped, crept slowly forward, climbed back onto the pile of rocks. She peered down into the stump. Owyn's smudged, round face looked up from among the dragons. Baby dragons they were—none looked to be larger than a fox. Their heads, on long, slender necks, sprouted up like a cluster of mushrooms. Their eyes all gleamed at her.

Lyf wrenched her gaze from the dráclings and whispered urgently to Owyn. "Grab my hand. Quick! I'll pull you out!"

"Why?" Owyn asked, then was convulsed with a spasm of coughing.

"Just do as I say!"

Lyf reached down into the stump, pushing the egg to one side so as not to squash it. Slowly. Slowly. Don't alarm the draclings.

"No!" Owyn said. "You come in here. It's warm!"

"Owyn!" Lyf forced herself to keep her arm stretched down. One of the draclings sniffed at her hand, then flicked at it with a forked tongue. Lyf snatched it away.

"Owyn!" she said, soft and urgent. "Come here! Take my hand!"

She was reaching down to him again when she felt something bright, something fizzy, something tingly in her mind.

<Hungry.>

She had not *heard* it, yet it was as clear to her as speech. Every fiber in her body ached to pull back, to climb down off the stump, to run through the forest and away. Yet something held her, some force of concentration. Like a bird kenning it was, but more knowing, more aware. It did not suck her *in*to itself—only made itself known. And a chorus arose—a silent, plaintive chorus that tickled at her mind: <Hungry. Hungry. Hungry.>

The draclings surged toward her, a dark wave in the pit of the stump.

"Owyn, *now!* They're hungry!"

"I'm hungry too."

"They might put it in mind to eat *you*."

"They won't." Owyn sounded certain. And truly they did not seem interested in Owyn—but with Lyf it was elsewise. They crowded below her within the stump, clambering one on top of another, lunging at her, all the while pelting her mind with their incessant *hungries*.

It was too much. Lyf scrambled off the rock pile to the ground. The egg thumped hard against her stomach. She ran a few steps, stopped, ran a few steps more, stopped again.

It wasn't fair that this had happened. She *couldn't* rescue Owyn. She was only a child herself.

But . . .

She couldn't run away. She couldn't leave him alone with those draclings.

Plague him! Lyf kicked a tree, then recoiled from the pain in her toes. Why hadn't he taken her hand? They could have been well away by now—not *far* away, but at least out of the draclings' sight.

She had wanted to see a dracling, but this . . . There were eight or nine of them at least within that stump—perhaps a score. And Kaeldra gone . . .

They were perilous, Kaeldra had said. Even the babies—though winsome they could be. And yet they had never harmed Kaeldra, save for a few unintended scratches and burns.

<Hungry.>

Lyf looked up sharply. A dracling head poked over the edge of the stump, looking down at her. The head cocked to one side, as if curious. Another head popped above the rim—and then another. One snorted out a filmy smoke puff.

<Hungry. Hungry. Hungry.>

A flood of longing, stronger than spoken words, tugged at her.

They were babies, only babies. And they hadn't harmed Owyn. And their mothers had been killed—surely these were the selfsame draclings Kaeldra had sought.

But she had no food; they would give her no peace.

"Lyf?" Owyn's voice came from within the stump. "Will you *come?* It's *warm!*"

It would be nice to be warm. The chill night air pierced through Lyf's kirtle and cloak. Perhaps, she thought, the draclings would settle down when they found she had no food.

Lyf dangled the egg in its carrier down into the stump to Owyn, then gingerly climbed in herself. The draclings surged around her, prodding her with their snouts, nuzzling her for all the world like ponies looking for apples. She could not see them well in the darkness—only the gleamings of their eyes and the long, narrow shapes of their snouts. She held still, not wanting to affright them.

A ripping noise; one had nipped at her tunic. "No!" Lyf said. The dracling snorted out a wisp of smoke. Its breath felt warm and smelled . . . of what? Porridge, burnt to the pot?

Now they all pressed closer, hooking their needle-sharp talons into her cloak, pelting her mind with their pitiful *hungries*. They seemed to be going for her stomach. They all wanted to nuzzle her stomach.

Understanding hit with a jolt. They wanted milk! They thought *she* was a mother! "No!" Lyf cried, jerking back. "Get away! No!"

The draclings froze, startled. One breathed out a tiny lick of flame.

Gingerly, Lyf lay down, curled herself tightly about Owyn. They could not reach him now—nor her stomach. Behind her she heard shuffling noises. She felt their snouts poking at her back, felt their breath-warmth seeping in through her clothes. <Hungry,> came a voice in her head. Then an overlapping of <Hungry> and <hungry> and <hungry.> Soon the chorus dwindled, but their cravings still wafted through Lyf's mind. They seemed so forlorn that she longed to turn round and comfort them. But then they would only harangue her for milk. If Mama could see her now . . .

But Lyf could not imagine it. She was so far beyond the ills that Mama feared for her—the petty bruises and scrapes, the short forays into the wood for kindling. Mama seemed far away, part of another life. She seemed not altogether *real*.

It was warm inside the stump. Lyf inhaled the rich commingled scents of damp wool and rotting wood, of rain-washed fir and draclings' smoky breath. Owyn coughed once in her arms, then snuggled close against her. His breath came deep and slow.

Lyf slept—and woke but once, at false dawn, surrounded by a throbbing, liquid vibration. Like the purr of a byre cat, only louder. Kaeldra had spoken of this, Lyf mused sleepily. What had she called it?

Oh, yes.

Thrumming. She called it thrumming.

It was raining when Lyf awoke.

She knew it before she opened her eyes—by the prick of tiny droplets on leaves, by the fresh rain smell in the air. Yet she was warm, all-over warm. Her body melted into the curves of the ground, and a heavy, warm blanket enveloped her.

Lyf yawned, stretched. Something flopped off her arm; her eyes flew open.

Draclings. Sleeping draclings all around. They curled in the hollow of her back, draped across her hips, nestled into the space behind her knees.

And all the past day's events came flooding back: Kaeldra and Jeorg taken, betrayed by Nysien; the long trek through the forest; the hunger . . .

She felt it now, the hard gnawing of hunger in her belly. Slowly she sat up, careful not to disturb the sleeping draclings.

A soft gray light filtered down. The rain was sparse; little made its way past the overhanging branches to splash inside the stump. Lyf glanced about for Owyn. Still sleeping. He lay snuggled between two draclings as if they were his own brothers and sisters. His back rose and fell in sleep breathing, as did the draclings' backs. All throughout the stump they did so: massed together in a tangled heap that rose in some places as it fell in others, each to the rhythm of its own breath's pulse. Smoke rose in filmy wisps from some of the draclings' nostrils; others made faint, fluttery whistlings as they slept.

It was strange and marvelsome to watch.

Lyf tried to count them now while they slept, tried to sort out the welter of heads and backs and legs and tails. Eleven heads she found, though likely there were more, tucked beneath tails and backs and taloned feet. Most of the draclings were muted reds or greens—some mottle-hued, others of a single even tone. The reds were males and the greens females—Kaeldra had told her this. But the littlest draclings were covered with yellow-tan skins that fit them all wrinkly and loose.

Lyf reached out with a finger and gently stroked the back of one of the littler ones. It felt soft and almost powdery, like the wings of a moth. Beneath, Lyf thought she could see a tint of bluish green. The dracling, still sleeping, kneaded the air with its knobbly yellow talons—more like birds' feet than animal claws.

The bigger draclings must have shed their skins, Lyf surmised. Their throats and underbellies were supple and leathery, but everywhere else they were covered with scales.

Not hard and metallic, as Lyf had imagined them, but softer, translucent, like fingernails.

The smallest draclings looked to be the size of puppies; the largest, the size of full-grown foxes. All were long and lean, like stoats, with tapered, lizardy tails and narrow snouts that bulged out at the end near their nostrils. Down each dracling's neck and back and tail ran a soft, leathery ridge.

And wings! All but the littlest ones had wings—flimsy, folded membranes, thinner than vellum. Lyf touched one; the dracling twitched its tail like a skittish cat. On the smallest draclings' backs, where the others had wings, were two hard, bony knobs. Wing buds. Kaeldra had told her of these, as well.

<Hungry.>

A big, orangy-red dracling was staring at her now from the far side of the stump. His eyes were all-over green, save for a black slit at the center of them. Intelligent eyes.

Lyf put a finger to her lips. "Sh," she said.

But the others were waking, raising their heads.

<Hungry. Hungry.>

"No," Lyf said, "I have no food. I can't—" But they paid her no mind. They untangled themselves one by one, wriggling, trampling on one another, stumbling across the stump to Lyf. She tried to scoot away, but only roused another dracling behind her, who joined the others in nudging at her stomach with its snout.

<Hungry.>

A green dracling nipped at Lyf's kirtle and tore it; when Lyf gently pushed her away, the dracling huffed out an indignant cloud of smoke.

Then Owyn was stretching, yawning. He regarded the

draclings without surprise, then coughed and turned to Lyf. "I'm hungry!" he said.

"You're not alone," she said crossly, shielding her stomach with one hand and shoving away the prodding snouts of draclings with the other. But she was surrounded; they poked her unmercifully, pelted her ceaselessly with their *hungries*. One of the littlest ones started nibbling at her fingers. Lyf could bear it no longer. She jumped up, grabbed Owyn by the waist, and hoisted him to the top of the stump. She climbed up after. "Let's go," she said.

"Why?" Owyn did not budge.

"For food."

"Oh." Owyn slid down the boulders to the ground; Lyf followed. Chilly. It was chilly. She took Owyn's hand and tried to run, but he stopped again. "Aren't we waiting for the draclings?"

"No! We can't feed them, too. We'd never find enough."

"Why?"

"We just wouldn't, Owyn. Now come!" A dracling's head appeared at the top of the stump, and another and another. Then the whole horde of them appeared, surging over the top....

"Stay!" Lyf cried.

They stilled, stared at her. Lyf gaped.

They had understood her. They had *obeyed.*

She shooed Owyn along the track, but she herself walked backward, facing the draclings. "Stay," she told them. "I'll bring food soon. Now, stay."

"But they're hungry," Owyn said.

As if she didn't know. "They can find food for themselves. They can hunt."

"What if they're too little to hunt?"

"Yanil will have food. We'll tell him where they are."

"How will he *find* them?"

Lyf wasn't even sure how she was going to find Yanil, but she didn't tell Owyn. The track had forked some way back. But she had to leave the draclings, or they would poke her to death.

One dracling edged forward over the rim of the stump.

"Stay!" Lyf ordered.

It blew out a puff of blue smoke. <Hungry.>

"Stay!"

"You forgot about the egg," Owyn said.

The egg. She *had* forgotten it. Well, she would tell Yanil about that as well. She would tell him everything, and leave all in his hands. *I trust him completely*, Kaeldra had said, *and so must you*.

Lyf stumbled backward, commanding the draclings to stay, until the track took a twist and the stump disappeared behind a clump of bushes. Then, "Quick, Owyn. Run!" she said and, flinging a last, desperate "Stay!" over her shoulder, grabbed Owyn's hand and bolted.

Scratching sounds behind her. Rustlings. <Hungries> pelted at her mind, like a hail of pebbles.

"Run, Owyn. Faster!" The draclings were babies; perhaps they were slow. Lyf looked back and saw the whole pack of them behind, rounding the bend in the track. They didn't seem to be able to fly but . . . they were *fast*.

"Run!"

It was no use. One dracling brushed against her boots, and then another, and then they were surging all about her, thrumming, rubbing against her legs. She tripped, sprawled out in the dirt. There was a ripping sound; sharp pain pierced her knee.

<Hungry. Hungry. Hungry.>

Draclings swarmed over her, nuzzling at her back, her neck, her legs, beneath her arms. "Stop it!" Lyf said. "I don't have any food! Not in me and not out of me." The tears started at the backs of her eyes and just kept on coming. "And Kaeldra's gone and she might be hurt and I miss my mama and the hunters are looking for us and my knee pains me and you ripped my kirtle and I'm *hungry*! *I'm* hungry too!" Now the sobs were coming; they engulfed her words and racked her chest. She gave herself up to them, pressed her face into the dirt, and wept.

Lyf wept until she was all wept out, until there were no tears left within her. Through her last, quavery sobs, she was dimly aware that she no longer heard the draclings. She no longer *felt* them. They weren't poking at her now.

Lyf wiped her face on her sleeve, looked up.

A ring of draclings surrounded her, heads cocked quizzically to one side. Owyn moved toward her, patted her head as if she were a favorite dog. "There now, Auntie Lyf," he said. "There now."

Lyf snuffled, breathed in a ragged breath.

Well. They were together now—all of them—until they reached Yanil's farm.

Then *he* would shoulder the load.

Harper's Tale

They were not taken to the dungeon—Kaeldra and Jeorg and this most excellent of harpers. They were feted with meats and pastries, and put up in comfort. But iron bars barricaded the window, and guards stood outside the door.

They were led into the presence of the queen, who was soft with them until they refused to lead her to dragons, and then became hard. Angry, she returned them to the barred and guarded room.

And one of the bars was loose.

Chapter 8

Sign of the Dove

They were all day trekking through the forest. Lyf went back for the egg, then made her way east as well as she could. Rain squalls came and went, but often, between them, golden shafts of light pierced the canopy of needlecone trees, showing the direction of the sun. It was quiet, save for scattered birdcalls and the sounds of their own making. Lyf's fears of bounty hunters and soldiers, of wolves and holt cats receded to an anxious niggling at the edges of her mind. She had enough to fret about with trying to find Yanil—and food. The craving in her belly was constant and, even if she could have forgotten her own hunger, Owyn and the draclings never let her forget theirs.

When they weren't plaguing her for food, the draclings romped through the underbrush, flushing out birds and stripemonks and twitchmice. Their falconlike talons seemed too big for their bodies. Like puppies. They ran like puppies too, Lyf thought—stiffly, clumsily, and yet with an odd buoyant lightness to their gait. Though they often flapped their wings, never did she see them fly—or even attempt it. They thrashed in playful skirmishes, nipping, clouting with their tails, huffing out clouds of sparks and smoke. Once Lyf marked a tiny lick of blue flame out of the corner of her eye; she turned to see fire winking along a low grapebush branch. Quickly she stomped it out, scolding the draclings. Thank the heavens all was sodden, or they might set the forest ablaze! She worried too that some of them might get hurt in this rough play, might be burned or bitten or clawed. Yet none seemed to come to harm. They walked away from their battles swaggering like byre cats who've caught a mouse—tremendously pleased with themselves.

Lyf fretted more for Owyn, who had no fear of the draclings and *would* join in their play, despite Lyf's scoldings and pleadings. The draclings seemed to tolerate him; never did they willfully nip or thrash him. Still, Owyn received his share of inadvertent thumpings, and more than once was knocked flat. From time to time he found a stick and shook it at them, shouting. The draclings fled crashing into the bushes, then peered out between the leaves. Lyf wondered if they were humoring him. She wondered if they spoke to Owyn, too, but when she asked him about it, he only held his head and said, "It sparkles!" At least they seemed to have helped his throatill. He still coughed fitfully, but not nearly so often as before his night in the warm.

How the draclings had survived for so long without their mothers, Lyf did not know. Though often they bounded after small forest creatures, only twice, in Lyf's seeing, did they catch one. And that was not near enough food. Of birds they took no notice; once a whitchil lit on a dracling's back ridge, but never a move did he make to catch it.

They disdained the few half-ripe corberries Lyf found, and refused as well the stray milgrum cloves she dug up. But once, they nosed out a nest of chirp bugs and bounded after the hopping insects, crunching happily whenever they caught one. Another time, Lyf found a store of nuts in a tree bole—a hoard of some squirrel gone from its nest. She was sharing these with Owyn when the draclings came romping toward her. They knocked the nuts out of Lyf's hands, captured them in their talons, devoured them shells and all. Their teeth were small and thickly set, sharper than needles at their tips. Lyf and Owyn could only watch helplessly, fearing for their fingers.

Lyf tried to count the draclings and came out with a different tally each time. At last she counted thirteen three times running—and deemed that close enough. They did not all look to be the same age. Jeorg had said, now Lyf remembered, that they came from different clutches. The three small, byre cat-sized draclings were covered in the soft skins Lyf had marked before. In full daylight, she could see that the skins were split in places, and tiny scales showed through. She guessed that they would soon shed. Then there was a middle group of six, who seemed nearly of an age. They were mottle-hued, in sundry shades of red and green. The four fox-sized draclings seemed eldest. Their scales, more even in tone than those of the others, glittered in the shifting forest light. The hard, bony ridges above their eyes made them look comically fierce.

Lyf wearied as the day wore on. The egg hung heavy on

her neck and made it ache. Often Owyn would stop, refusing to go on unless she carried him, and she would lug him as far as she could. She still tried to take her bearings from the slanting of the sun shafts between showers and so wend their way to the east. But the branches wove an ever tighter fabric overhead, and the lower she came down the mountain, the thicker grew the new foliage. Spring had come earlier here than at home. Soon, the forest was filled with a watery green light that gave no hint as to direction.

And ever she was hungry.

She walked slowly now, uncertain of her course. East of the mountains, Kaeldra had said. But that covered a lot of land. Lyf set down the egg and climbed up into a tree, admonishing Owyn not, on pain of death, to budge. She pulled herself up onto a low bough, then climbed higher, branch to branch, until the boughs would no longer support her. She could see farther here; the branches webbed more thinly across the sky. Yet still, it was all trees. Only trees.

No—wait.

Something gray across the sky—a faint, twisting thread of woodsmoke. Lyf strained to see whence it arose and thought she made out a clearing in the distance. It must be a clearing, she thought. It must be Yanil's farm. *Had* to be.

It was not terribly far, that smoke. And it arose from nearly due east.

It was twilight when they came to the clearing. Lyf was listless from hunger, bone-weary from the hard-slogging walk. A blister on her left heel smarted; a bruise on her right knee ached. Owyn had cried to be carried more and more often; the egg seemed to grow ever heavier until it hung like an anvil from her neck. The smallest draclings lagged far behind—all but a little one who had hooked her talons into the weave of Lyf's cloak and climbed up onto her shoulders. A female it was—Lyf could tell by the greeny-blue scales that peeked out through the rents in its hide. The dracling was surprisingly light, and warmed Lyf's neck. But when its long tail wasn't whipping about, pummeling Lyf's arms, the little dracling was nuzzling in close, breathing smoke in Lyf's face. *She's going to set my hair afire, I know it,* Lyf thought. She had tried gently to shrug the dracling off, but the little one only dug in with her talons, piercing clear through cloak and kirtle to bare skin. At last Lyf had given up trying to dislodge her and had wound the dracling's tail like a muffler about her neck.

Lyf waited at the edge of the wood until all of the draclings had straggled in. Across the field in the fading gray light she could make out the byre and a few outlying sheds.

And a dovecote. There was a dovecote.

Beyond lay the cottage, its smoke a tantalizing promise of food and rest and warmth.

Yanil would take care of her, Kaeldra had said.

If this *was* Yanil's cottage.

If only, Lyf thought, she could leave the draclings here in the woods while she checked the lintel for the dove sign.

"Stay!" she said to them.

She hefted Owyn to one hip and set out across the field. "Stay!"

The draclings thronged after her, thrumming and rubbing against her legs.

"Stay!"

They came crowding round her feet, not even pretending to obey.

Lyf sighed. She had feared it would come to this. She could not escape them.

What now?

The cottage looked so snug, so solid. A yellow glow flickered in the window, spilled out across the yard.

It *must* be Yanil's cottage. Farms with dovecotes were few enough—and this stood just east of the mountains. At any pass, the darkness was thickening. Likely none would see them crossing the field. She would check the lintel and knock only if the sign of the dove was there.

She trudged across the furrowed field—Owyn on one hip, the egg in its carrier before her, one dracling draped around her neck, a dozen more slinking behind. The rain had started up again—and hard. A cold stream trickled down her back; she was sodden to the bone. She skirted the byre and made straight for the cottage.

There. A mark above the lintel. A dove?

Yes. She could make it out now. A dove!

Lyf stumbled eagerly forward, grasped the iron knocker, thudded at the door. The dracings crowded round; she let Owyn slide down her hip to the ground. She could smell the fire and the rich aroma of a well-spiced, meaty stew.

Footsteps. The door was thrust ajar; a lanky, sandy-haired youth peered out. He looked older than Lyf, though not by much.

"We're here for Yanil—" she began, then stopped, silenced by the shock in his eyes.

"Begone with you!" he said, urgent and low. "And take your beasties with you. We're not wantin' you here.

"Begone!"

Harper's Tale

A man does not suspect, when he goes to a great deal of trouble to do a thing secretly, that those from whom he hides his deed might have planned it all along.

The window was high, my lords and ladies. The ground was far below. Were it not for the blankets, which the captives ripped into strips and knotted together, they would never have escaped.

That the queen might have left the blankets for just such a purpose . . . what reasonable soul would suspect?

Also I would think that if the queen truly desired her captives' escape, she might have had the courtesy to loosen *two* bars instead of one, so that harpers, grown stout from the gains of their excellence, would not have to writhe and squirm and wriggle most painfully to squeeze out.

(Would you pass me one of those tarts? There's a good lass!)

Perhaps the late arrival of Nysien in the room should have set their thumbs to pricking. But he was blackened in one eye and raging against the Krags. And it was he, after all, who discovered the loose bar. Why, if he had betrayed them, would he help them to flee?

So they put their suspicions to rest.

And Kaeldra, Jeorg, Nysien, and the finest harper since the time of the old road builders escaped and stole away.

Chapter 9

Brine Rats

"Gar? Gar, who is it?" A woman's voice came from within the cottage.

"It's no one, Ma. Just . . ."

The door opened wider, and a short, round, worried-looking woman peered out. Wisps of gray hair escaped her headwrap. She was haloed in yellow light. Something shifted in her face; she drew in breath. Lyf felt a quick movement near her feet, then looked down to see a long, red tail streaking through the doorway and into the cottage.

Screams from within. More streaking forms: the draclings.

"Come back!" Lyf cried, but to no avail. The overpowering flood of their hunger surged into her mind.

The youth named Gar tried to shove the door shut, but a tangle of draclings and skirt and leg got in the way. The little bluish green female on Lyf's shoulders gathered herself, leapt, thudded against the door, then staggered back, shook herself, and tunneled under the woman's skirts.

Gar had vanished from the doorway, and now the woman fled within as well, leaving the door ajar. With a hoarse shout, Owyn bolted through.

"Owyn!" Lyf snatched at the nape of his cloak, missed, lunged after him into the cottage.

All was in an uproar.

Draclings filled the room, scrambling over one another to fling themselves at a large, steaming kettle that hung over a central hearth. They pumped their wings futilely, as if trying to fly. Two of the larger draclings stretched up on hind legs until their talons hooked over the rim. The kettle tilted precariously. The heat of the iron surface didn't seem to trouble them, but then one stepped into the fire, sprang sharply back, knocked over the churn. Milk came gushing out. A dark-haired girl leapt upon a bench, screaming. Another, younger, girl ventured into the fray and swatted at the draclings with a broom. She was screaming too. The woman grabbed hold of the broom-swatting girl's waist and strove to drag her away. The youth, from a safe distance, pelted the draclings with crab apples.

Lyf looked about for Owyn. There! He had somehow got hold of a barley bannock and was happily munching away.

"Come! Draclings, come!" Lyf called.

They still paid her no mind, except for one of the littlest ones, who stretched up on his hind legs and tried to nibble Lyf's fingers. An apple smacked against a big orangy-red dracling's head. He whipped around, spat out a lick of blue flame. It kindled at one edge of the broom straw and then—to Lyf's horror—set it all ablaze.

With an ear-piercing shriek, the girl dropped the broom, then retreated back near her sister. The woman, surprisingly quick, snatched up a ewer and dumped water onto the broom. In a billow of steam, the fire hissed out.

The draclings stared raptly at the smoldering broom. For a moment all was silent, save for the last fizzling hiss of steam. One by one, they all—the bench-standing girl and the broom-swatting girl, the youth named Gar and the woman who must be their mother—turned to look at Lyf.

She felt the weight of their gazes upon her. "I'm sorry," she said. "They're hungry. And Owyn, too. I'm sorry he took your bread. We are all of us—" She stopped, flustered. "This *is* ... where Yanil lives?"

"Aye, 'tis," the woman said. "Only ..." She paused. "We're not knowing where he is. I'm afeared—" She drew breath, spoke again. "But I need to know this: Will they harm us? The beasties?"

"Owyn and I, we spent the night with them—and all this day past. And never have they made shift to harm us. But ... they *are* hungry."

"Alone in the woods with 'em? Poor lass! And you not more than ten winters old, by the look of you."

"Almost twelve," Lyf said. She hated it when people thought she was younger than she was. Which they did. Ever they did. And she thought, when she was truthful with herself, that it was not only her smallness, but something else as well. Something that had been protected which, in most children of her age, had been buffeted about a bit. Something cosseted and soft.

The woman regarded Lyf thoughtfully. Her flesh was slack, with many fine wrinkles, but her eyes looked keen and alert. She seemed about to say something when a *thud* by the kettle drew her eye. The draclings were assailing it again.

"Fetch the brine rats from the byre, Gar! And be quick about it!"

"But *Ma*—"

"Fetch them then, Gar! We are doing this thing. Your da has pledged himself—pledged all of us. Get along with you!"

Gar sullenly turned and loped out the doorway.

The woman turned to Lyf. "Can you spoon them out a bit of the stew? To keep them busy till the brine rats are come?"

"Yes," Lyf said. But . . . brine rats. What *were* these brine rats?

Lyf shrugged off the egg carrier, set it down in a corner. The woman handed her a ladle and a wide wooden basin. Lyf made her way into the swarm of draclings near the pot, careful not to step on talon or tail, and hoping not to get nipped. They crowded round her, nosing her. Their *hungries* swelled to a flood in her mind. She breathed in the rich, meaty aroma and scooped high over the pot so that the draclings could not reach the basin. They leaped up, nipping with needle-sharp teeth.

Lyf set down the basin; the draclings fell into a slurping frenzy, pushing it across the rush-strewn floor. She hoped the woman would offer *her* "a bit of the stew" as well. And Owyn too, of course. Although, she thought enviously, he was still munching on his loaf. His stomach was no longer hollow, like hers.

"Gar bears a long grudge, so he does," the woman said, staring anxiously at the draclings. "All the way from the last time."

"The last time?"

"When the other green-eyed one came," the bench-standing girl said.

"Her that was dressed like a boy," the broom-swatting girl said.

"You mean Kaeldra?" Lyf asked.

The woman nodded. "Aye, she's the one. Though she called herself Coldran." She eyed Lyf sharply. "And who would *you* be, then?"

"Lyf. Kaeldra's second-sister. And this is Owyn, Kaeldra's son."

Owyn looked up from his loaf. "Is Mama here?"

Lyf shook her head. Owyn's face fell. Lyf feared that he would cry, but he only took another bite of bannock.

"But Yanil . . . will be back, then?" she asked the woman. She *needed* for him to come back.

"He's my husband. He will come back—unless harm has befallen him."

The broom-swatting girl edged toward the draclings. One of them looked up and snorted out smoke. The girl hastened back.

"What happened . . . the last time . . . with Gar?" Lyf asked.

"Didn't the other one tell you? Those draclings ate three of Gar's pet rabbits. That was bad enough. But t'other thing . . . They killed our dog."

"Burnt it to a cinder," the broom-swatting girl said.

"Oh!" Lyf was taken aback.

"But you must know how the beasties are, being a dragon girl yourself."

"I'm *not* a dragon girl. I don't care a crumb about the draclings! They followed us here; we couldn't get rid of them!"

Gar pushed through the door and thumped down two heavy buckets on the floor. A greenish liquid came sloshing over the sides. Furry, green-gray lumps floated within.

"What's that?" Lyf asked.

"Why, brine rats," the woman said. "What did you think?"

"But what . . . what *are* brine rats?"

The woman seemed surprised. "You of all folk should know. We trap our rats and pickle them in brine. It's for to feed the beasties, should they have need. All of the dove sign do it."

Pickled rats? Ugh! All at once, Lyf felt queasy.

The draclings looked up, sniffing. "Let's fetch these down to the cellar now," the woman said. "I will not turn the beasties out, but I won't be havin' them skelterin' all about the place." She lugged the pails to the cellar hatch, pried it open.

"Are you certain they won't do harm to the draclings? Those brine rats?" Lyf asked.

"It's meat, missy—only meat! That's what they like—or so my Yanil tells me."

Two of the draclings edged toward the buckets. The basin, Lyf saw, was licked clean. The woman grabbed one bucket and climbed down the ladder. Lyf took hold of the second bucket, waited to hand it down.

<Hungry.> The two draclings were nuzzling at the bucket.

"Wait," Lyf said. "In a moment."

The other draclings looked up. A few of them stepped tentatively toward Lyf, then they all scampered in a pack across the room and converged about the bucket.

"Hurry!" the woman said. "Give it down!"

Lyf handed her the bucket. The draclings spilled through the hatch and down the ladder. Lyf heard the woman cry out, "Oh! Oh, me!" as she was swallowed up by a tide of draclings. Then she was charging back up the ladder, startlingly spry for her girth. "Shut the hatch!" she said. "Shut it!"

Lyf started to, but then stopped, troubled, and peered into the darkness below.

The larger draclings thronged all around the buckets—but the three littlest ones couldn't get near. They couldn't push their way in to eat. One of them nipped at the other draclings' tails, spitting out sparks.

They hadn't been able to get at the stew, either. And in the forest . . . had they eaten then? Lyf couldn't recall.

"Would you shut that hatch!" the woman was saying. "I'll ladle you out some stew!"

Lyf could feel their *hungries* now—just a few of them—high and plaintive. Her own stomach growled. "The little ones," she said. "They can't get to the food. I'll have to feed them."

She climbed down the ladder into the damp, low-ceilinged cellar, pushed her way through the mob of draclings. The brine rats reeked of vinegar and pickling spices and something else—a sickening, rancid-meat smell. Lyf approached one of the buckets, careful not to get too near those needle-sharp teeth. She steeled herself and reached within, shuddering at the slimy touch of pickled rat fur. She groped round until she found a tail, then, grasping it between thumb and forefinger, pulled it out. In the half-light from above she could see the dead rat's wide-open eyes, the glimmer of a pointy tooth. Ugh! She flung it back among the little draclings. The spark spitter reared up, caught it in his mouth, gobbled it with a crunch and a gulp. Lyf tossed out one rat after another, until the little ones had eaten their fill.

Abruptly, she glimpsed movement from above. Something smacked her square in the face, then bounced onto the floor.

A brine rat! Revolted, she wiped her eyes and looked up into Gar's smirking face.

"Dragon girl," he taunted.

Tears sprang into Lyf's eyes. She was *not*. She had only brought them here, and now Yanil would do what needed to be done with them. But . . . how if Yanil never came?

"Gar!" The woman's voice was angry. "Tell the lass you're sorry or you'll be feelin' the back of my hand."

Gar's face disappeared from the hatch.

"Gar! *Gar!*"

Scuffling footsteps above, and then the slam of the door.

Now all the brine rats were gone. Some of the draclings had tipped over the buckets and were snuffling about inside them, pushing them across the cellar floor until they bumped against the rows of kegs, the baskets of roots and dried peas. Their bellies bulged and sagged. One by one, the draclings stretched, yawned, curled up together until they formed a lumpy mass. Lyf started for the ladder, but the three littlest draclings sprang up and thronged about her feet, thrumming. And she felt a plea, a tugging at her mind: <Stay.>

"Lyf?" The woman and two girls were peering down at her. "Come have some stew now," the woman said. "You've done your part."

<Stay.> The draclings rubbed against her legs.

Reluctantly, Lyf bent down, scratched each of their heads in turn. They were thrumming now, thrumming deep in their throats. One, whose scales showed the color of green apples through rents in her tattered skin, nibbled gently at Lyf's fingers. The little bluish green-scaled dracling hooked her talons into Lyf's gown and tried to climb up. Lyf backed away fast, shaking her off. The pumpkin-colored one spat out sparks.

"You stay here," Lyf ordered, and added, "I'll soon return."

<*Stay.*> It was a plaintive chorus in Lyf's mind, nearly impossible to resist.

Lyf hardened herself, climbed briskly up the ladder, and shut the hatch.

She was *not* the dragon girl.

"I thought you didn't like them."

The younger of the two sisters poured water over Lyf's hands. Lyf scrubbed hard, trying to get rid of the brine rats' stench.

"You said you didn't care about them, but you went down to feed the little ones. And then you stroked them, as if they were only byre cats. You looked like you might be listening to them. Like you can understand them. *Can* you?"

"I don't know," Lyf said shortly, wiping her hands on her kirtle. They still stank, but she had cleaned them as best she could.

"Leave her be now, Brita," the woman said. "It's late. Go to the loft with your sister and get you to bed."

"But Ma!"

"Begone with you!"

Brita left grudgingly, moving slowly up the ladder, with many a lingering look back.

The woman handed Lyf a warm bowl of stew. It was thick and meaty and good. Lyf ate until the pangs in her stomach subsided and then, to the gentle proddings of the woman—her name was Una—she poured out her tale. Una was easy to talk to, now they were alone. Owyn had eaten while Lyf fed the draclings and lay asleep, hugging the egg.

Gar had not returned. But Lyf heard shiftings in the straw above, and she was all but certain that the two girls had their ears pressed to the boards.

"And what was it you were saying of Yanil?" Lyf asked when she had done with her story. "Why do you fear for him?"

Lamplight flickered across Una's face, and Lyf saw in it now the worried look she had marked before. "He left early in the day with our two youngest boys and the dog. He was carting a mite of our brew to the tavern, he said. He would be home afore sunset, he said. And we haven't seen him since."

"Maybe he stayed for supper," Lyf suggested hopefully.

"Maybe. But those soldiers who came through, pillaging for food? They nearly sacked the place. I don't think they saw the brine rats, but if they did . . ."

Lyf was confused. "Would that be bad?"

"'Tis a sure sign we're aiding the dragons, lass! We can't be feedin' them our stock, you know. We keep the brine rats in an old, dry well and draw them up in buckets. I didn't see the soldiers look there. But they looked at the dovecote long and hard. Suspicious—so they were. And the neighbors are distrustful of all of Yanil's comings and goings. And once my youngest son let slip something about brine rats." Una shook her head. "No. You can't be staying here now."

"But . . . Kaeldra said I could. She said Yanil would welcome us." Lyf swallowed hard.

"Child." Una laid a hand on Lyf's shoulder. "Your eyes—they're greener than green. There's no hidin' them."

But Lyf didn't *want* to leave. Kaeldra had said they should stay here. She had said Yanil would take care of them. Lyf would ask *him* when he returned.

Una sighed. "But where you will go, I can't say. My Yanil, he doesn't tell us about his friends among the dove sign. Some things aren't safe to know." She sighed again. She looked haggard now, and old. "I've no quarrel with you," she said at last. "But it's often I wish Yanil had nothing to do with the dove sign. It is hard—what with fearin' the soldiers, and fearin' our neighbors, and fearin' we might let something slip."

Then why didn't you send us away? Lyf wondered, afraid to ask.

But Una, as if reading her mind, said, "I couldn't just turn you away, now, could I? You and the little lad. There's no place safe for you—save here.

"But you can't be staying long. No. You must away again—and soon."

Lyf bedded down with Owyn and the egg on a straw pallet near the cellar hatch. "In case you should need to hide," Una said. Gar never did return, but Una went to spy him out and found him sleeping in the byre.

Lyf drowsed fitfully; not even the warm vibration of the egg could comfort her. One worry after another roused her all the night through: that Yanil would not return to take care of them, that Una would send them away, that harm had come to Kaeldra, that the soldiers would come knocking at the door, that the draclings would become restless in the cellar and burn through the hatch.

It was silent in the cottage, and yet whenever Lyf woke, she was aware of an awake presence. She looked round each time to see Una's dark form outlined against the window.

At last Lyf roused to the sound of voices. Soft, peach-colored light seeped in through the shutters. Lyf rolled over, saw the door swing open, and then Una was throwing herself into the arms of a tall, gray-haired man. *Yanil.* Lyf felt relief surging through her. *He would take care of them now.* Two boys crowded round; Una hugged each in turn. A shaggy dog shot into the room, sniffed around Lyf and Owyn.

Then, "Da! You're come!" And the two daughters came bounding down from the sleeping loft, flung themselves at the man.

The dog was sniffing at the hatch now, growling. It barked.

"Take Pekla out, Hof!" Una said. "Take her out!"

The man, looking over his daughters' shoulders, caught sight of Lyf. He started, visibly. "By the sun's blessed rays," he whispered. He released the girls, took one slow step forward, then turned to Una. "Are they here, then?" he asked. "The beasties?"

"In the cellar," she said.

The man turned back to Lyf. "So it's Lyf, is it? And Owyn there beside you?"

Lyf nodded.

"And glad I am to see you," Yanil said. "You're all the talk of Tyneth."

Harper's Tale

Why would a man betray his own wife's kin for gold?

For as many causes, my lords, as there are traitors.

Nysien had been raised as a cosseted, petty prince—proud of his lands, proud of his gold, proud of the honor he was granted on account of them.

*Over*proud—if you want the truth of it, my ladies.

Then his mother ran off with the reeve. Nysien's father, fuddled with brew, lost lands and gold in a day to a Kragish warlord. Never mind that the Krags would have seized them in time, no matter how hard-fought the battle.

Kin had betrayed Nysien—now Nysien would betray kin.

Not out of malice to Kaeldra or Lyf, but only that he was nothing without his gold. He might even have persuaded himself that he would do his kin no harm.

What of his fabled rage against the Krags, you ask, my lord? Why would he conspire with his sworn foes?

He did rage against the Krags, but all the while seethed silently against his mother's and father's betrayals. And all the while yearned for his old prosperity.

Prosperity—and *honor*.

Folk did not *honor* him as before, my lord. This soured, curdled, festered within him.

He was an aggrieved soul and he could not unclench himself from his grievance and he could not see beyond it.

You should pity him, my lord (though *I* can't see my way to do it).

And what of Lyf, you ask, my lady?

Patience.

CHAPTER 10

Wolf's Head

All the talk of Tyneth?

"But I've never *been* to Tyneth! Who . . . ?" Lyf choked off her words, struck by a thought. "Kaeldra. Is she—"

"Last I heard, Kaeldra was well alive, child, and Jeorg with her."

"But . . . where is she? Did you see her? And who is talking of me?"

The man Yanil hesitated. His gray eyes, beneath shaggy, black brows, regarded her kindly. All were still now, watching her: the two boys, the two girls, Una. Owyn lay sleeping and did not rouse. "Sit down now, lass," Yanil said. "The boys and I are sore famished; a little bread and ale will put us all to rights. I'll tell you my tale while we break our fast—if you promise to tell me yours. And then, if it's well with you, I'd like to take a peek at those . . . those draclings of yours."

• • •

Yanil had not seen Kaeldra, as it happened, although all of Tyneth had been buzzing with rumors of her. "I heard tell she was captured by bounty hunters," he said.

Lyf nodded. "Betrayed by my sister's husband," she said, then leaned eagerly forward. "Did you see them?"

But no, he had not. He had heard they might be coming through Tyneth and had waited there long past dark, hoping to see Kaeldra, to find out what he might. But they never came.

"I don't know where she is," he said, "though I heard . . ."

"What? What did you hear?"

"I heard there's a wolf's head out on her. I heard they were taking her to the Kragish queen."

To the queen! Lyf was struck with the truth of this, though she had never dared think it before. And now she remembered what Yanil had said when first he had laid eyes on her. "You said . . . they were talking of *me*."

"Yes; the town's all ababble about a second green-eyed girl, younger than Kaeldra. I heard that you and the lad were left at a farm west of here, that you were safe at home with your mam, and that you had never been born. They're laying wagers on you at the inn, lass!" Yanil shook his head, suddenly grave. "I also heard—if you must know—that there's a wolf's head out on you. I fear they'll come searching after you—if they haven't already."

"You don't mean . . . here?" Lyf asked.

"Hereabouts. It'll come to *here* soon enough."

"Then it's *not* safe. We *can't* stay." Lyf felt all within her sag.

Yanil shook his head. He looked, Lyf thought, almost sad. "No," he said at last. "That you cannot."

• • •

The day passed in quiet talk and preparations. They must wait until dark to leave, Yanil said. "We can't risk the trek in daylight. I only hope the hunters go blundering about for a day or so before they think to come here." Lyf told her story again, and all listened, transfixed.

At the end of it Owyn woke, rubbed his eyes, stumbled across the room to Lyf. She drew him onto her lap; he buried his face in her chest, then peeked out at the strangers thronged round him. The girls soon lured him away, fussing over him, feeding him bits of cheese and apples, scrubbing his face, combing his hair—until he rebelled and fled to the loft.

"Can't we keep the lad here?" they implored, but Yanil firmly said no, explaining that he'd be safer elsewhere.

Yanil asked to see the dragon egg, then marveled over it, moving his callused fingers lightly over its ridged, yielding surface. "Do you hear the hum?" Lyf asked, and Yanil shook his head, looked wonderingly at her.

Before long they heard thumpings and scratchings from the cellar; the draclings were awake. Una feared they would get into the baskets of apples and roots, but Lyf told her they did not like them. Nonetheless, Yanil hauled in two more pails of brine rats from the byre. Gar was well, he said, but still sullen. Yanil had sent him out to cut bracken.

Now Yanil set the pails on the floor by the cellar hatch.

"Don't be lookin' at *me*," Una said. "I wouldn't go down there again for a bushel of gold croxains!"

"Let me feed them! Let me!" the boys begged.

"No!" Yanil said firmly, then, considering, asked, "Would they bite *me* do you think? Or flame at me?"

Lyf shrugged. "I can't speak for them. They do as they will."

"But you, then? Are you safe with them?"

"They won't harm me, I'm thinking."

And so she fed them again, hauling the buckets one by one down the ladder, then tossing rats to the little ones to ensure they wouldn't go hungry. Owyn scrambled down as well before any could stop him; Lyf scolded him, then relented and gave him some rats to toss.

The draclings were content to sleep again after they ate. Thank the heavens, Lyf thought. Yanil sent the children out to help Gar with the bracken, explaining to Lyf that there was a potter he knew who bought bracken fronds for packing. "It will give me a reason for the journey—and hide you and the beasties as well."

"Will the potter take care of us?" Lyf asked.

"Nay. There's another will do that—best not say who till you're needin' to know. But she's a decent soul."

"We can stay with her then—Owyn and me." It was a question, though Lyf had not phrased it so.

"Stay?" Yanil raised his shaggy black brows. "Well, the draclings, they must be goin' north. You know that, lass."

"Yes, but Owyn and I, we don't need to . . ." Lyf trailed off. Yanil scratched his chin, regarded her appraisingly. "Someone else can take the draclings, someone of the dove sign," Lyf finished.

Safe. She longed to be safe, to hand over the draclings and let someone else take up the burden. She ached to be *cared for* again.

But now, in Yanil's eyes she saw . . . disappointment? Had he hoped she'd be brave, like Kaeldra?

Lyf felt a twinge of bitterness against Kaeldra. Kaeldra was strong. She had always been strong, as long as Lyf had known her. But Kaeldra hadn't had the fever when she was young. Lyf wasn't the same as Kaeldra, and Yanil shouldn't expect her to be!

"You cannot stay long where I'm takin' you," Yanil said. "But . . ." He started to say something else, then seemed to think the better of it. His eyes ... in them she saw something ... was it pity?

And Lyf did not feel safe at all.

When it was nearly dark, Yanil hitched the mule to a cart heaped with bracken-fern and drew it up before the cottage. "There's brine rats beneath the bracken," Yanil said. "The beasties'll smell them, I'm thinking. But once they're done feeding, do you think you can make them stay?"

"They do as they will," Lyf said again, "not as I tell them." Yet often enough, she thought ruefully, they willed to stay with *her*.

Yanil boosted Owyn over the back of the cart, then made a stirrup with his hands for Lyf. She plunged into the deep, fragrant sea of new green fern. Yanil held out the egg; Lyf stood and slipped it into its carrier.

She watched Yanil stride within the cottage, holding two brine rats by their tails. The children were massed at the window, peering out. Then, "Now!" Yanil yelled, and Lyf called, "Come!"

She *felt* them before she saw them: a roiling in her mind, and now here they came, a dark wave within the cottage, bearing down fast. Yanil sprinted to the door and then, overtaken by the surge of draclings, hurled the brine rats into the cart. Lyf ducked, grabbed Owyn, thrashed her way back through the rustling ferns. Draclings came pouring in over the back rail, burrowed deep into the bracken, snuffled and snorted and slurped. Lyf hoped that all of them had come, but the evening light was dim, and they wriggled about until they were all entangled together—impossible to count.

"Are you well in there now Lyf?" Yanil called. "And Owyn? Are you?"

"Why?" Owyn asked, and Lyf said, "Well enough."

The cart lurched forward. Lyf rose to her knees and looked back. Dusk had fallen in the valley. Fog nestled among the trees like tufts of combed fleece. All were standing in the doorway now, haloed in the yellow glow from the cottage: Una, the two girls, the three boys. Lyf shyly raised her hand, and the others—all six of them—waved back. A surge of longing swept over her. If only she could be home and safe and cared for. Not cast out, with a wolf's head on her. Tears welled up in her eyes; she swiped them away. She watched until the cottage faded into darkness, then she sank back down into the bed of bracken.

The ferny-sweet fragrance muted the stench of the brine rats. Owyn yawned and snuggled close. Lyf stroked his hair. She could hear the draclings rustling about, could see curving, ridged backs and long, spiny tails emerge and disappear in the churning bracken.

She leaned back to rest. The bracken was soft, but scratchy. She touched the egg for comfort, but her mind refused to settle. Where were they bound? And where would they go after that? And when would they find refuge at last—someone to do what was needful for the draclings, someone else to take care of her and Owyn?

Lyf tipped her head back, watched the first pale stars glimmer out in the darkening sky. She wondered: Did Kaeldra see them too? Was she *alive*? Tears pricked again at Lyf's eyes; this time she let them come.

Something warm against her ear. A stench of brine. She turned to see a dracling—the big, orangy red one—eyeing her. Questioning.

Lyf hastily sat up and wiped away her tears. "It's no matter. I'm well enough," she said softly. The dracling cocked his head to one side. Lyf drew her fingers along his snout, up over the hard, bony ridge above his eyes. She scratched at the base of his leathery crest. The dracling nudged at her neck, thrumming.

And a word formed in her mind, a ticklish feeling above and between her ears.

<Skorch.>

"Skorch. Is that your *name*?"

<Skorch.>

A different voice—a *she* this time: <Kindle.> And another dracling was nudging her, the little one with the bluish green scales showing beneath her tattered hide. She hooked her talons into Lyf's sleeve and climbed up, settling about Lyf's shoulders.

"Oh, *you,* little one," Lyf said. "Your name is Kindle?"

<Kindle.>

Then a third dracling was clambering onto Lyf's lap, beside the egg—one of the middle-sized ones, mottled red.

<Smoak.>

"Hello, Smoak," Lyf said. She scratched behind his eye ridges. Smoak hiccuped, his breath reeking of brine.

Lyf wondered how they had come by their names. Perhaps from their mothers?

A thrumming arose now, louder and more rumbly than ever before. All around her, draclings poked their heads out of the bracken, *regarded* her.

Skorch nudged her cheek, and a questioning filled her mind.

<*I*?> Lyf asked. <*My* name?> She scanned the faces of the draclings all about her. She felt an expectancy, a waiting. She realized then that she had not spoken the words, but only *thought* them in a sending way.

<Lyf,> she told them. <I am called Lyf.>

• • •

Some way along, she fell asleep. It was hard to stay awake with the draclings warm and thrumming beside her. True, they wriggled at times, and often the one called Smoak hiccuped hot, brine-stinking breaths. Still, they were oddly comforting, these draclings.

Lyf roused once to a rustling noise, and saw Yanil raking heaps of bracken over the sleeping draclings. "All's well," he quickly assured her, "but you mustn't be seen." She checked Owyn—still asleep—then lay back and curled up between him and Kindle. A blanket of fragrant bracken swished over Lyf, blotting out the stars. And then the cart was bumping along again.

She woke at last to the sound of Yanil's whispered voice. "Lyf?"

She started to sit up, but Yanil said, "No, stay down—and keep the draclings still, if you can. I'll soon return."

And before she could ask where they were or whither he was going, she heard the crunch of his boots on dirt, and then a hollower tread—wooden steps—and the unmistakable creak of a hinge.

Something stirred in the bracken; Lyf felt a questioning in her mind. <Stay still,> she ordered. <All's well.>

Silence.

Owyn moaned, turned over, subsided into sleep.

Lyf listened hard to see if she could tell what sort of place they had come to. It was oddly quiet, and yet not completely so. She heard no chirp bugs, no wind stirring in leaves, no faraway bleatings of sheep. And yet she did hear the soft nickerings of horses. And somewhere, at a distance, water murmured. A river, she guessed, or a brook.

Something creaked. The hollow footsteps again. Then boots grating on dirt, and a whispered voice.

"Lyf. You can sit up now."

She did so, pushing the bracken fronds aside.

"There's an outer stair that gives onto a storeroom over the inn's stable," Yanil said. "Can you lead the draclings up?"

"The inn?" Lyf asked, her voice rising in alarm. "The inn where they were talking of me?" She could see it now: the high, gabled roof of the inn and, at the near end, the stable. They were in a courtyard, she saw.

"You will not enter the inn," Yanil assured her, "but only this one room that's set apart." Lyf made out a narrow, open stair, a landing above, and a shuttered window, which leaked yellow light. "You won't be here long. And there's one who will care for you here. One of the dove sign. Now, *can* you lead the beasties?"

Lyf nodded. She couldn't *stop* them from following her. She roused Owyn, brushed the bracken out of his hair, and told him to hush.

"Why?" he asked hoarsely.

"Just *hush*!"

Yanil lifted Owyn over the side of the cart, then held out his arms for her.

<Come,> Lyf summoned. <Come.> A half dozen dracling heads popped up out of the bracken.

<Come, Skorch; come, Smoak; come, Kindle.> It felt different when she called them by name. There was a jolt, a *connecting* in her mind.

Yanil helped Lyf out of the cart, careful not to squash the egg. Draclings surged silently over the side rail after her. She made for the stair. It was hard to place her feet aright on the treads in the dark—harder still because the egg blocked her view of her feet. She looked back and saw draclings following in a silent column behind her. Yanil had picked up Owyn and stood by the cart. She could hear him softly counting. ". . . ten, eleven, twelve, thirteen. That's the lot of 'em, then."

From the stable, she heard restless, horsey noises: snortings and stompings. Then suddenly a high, loud whinny. Lyf froze.

"Go on, then!" Yanil urged in a whisper. "Don't you be stopping!"

Above, Lyf saw the door swing ajar. Something poked out. It looked like . . . a joint of raw mutton.

It *was* a joint of mutton.

Lyf felt one of the draclings bump against the backs of her legs, saw a blur as it whizzed past her. Then another, and another—a stream of draclings bounding past her legs and up the stairs.

A muffled cry within. Lyf hastened up and through the doorway in time to see the mutton flying through the air. The draclings jumped at it, snapping their jaws. It bounced off a snout and landed near a side of raw mutton in the middle of the floor. The draclings set upon it, ravenous. Behind, Lyf heard Yanil's footsteps, heard the door quietly shut. She scanned the half-lit room to find who had thrown the mutton, and found her at last: a tall, big-boned woman watching wide-eyed from a shadowy corner.

"Oh dear," the woman said. "Oh dear."

"Alys," Yanil scolded softly, "I told you to wait for Lyf. Those beasties, they might have nipped off your fingers."

"I know," she said. She edged forward into the light of a lamp set on a cask. Her voice was sweet, and seemed too high to be coming from so large a woman. "But they looked so precious."

"Precious?" Yanil said. "Precious as wolves, they are—and far more perilous. Best you be leavin' the care of 'em to Lyf. And don't go feedin' them mutton."

"But those brine rats are *loathsome*! And my brother is wealthy—he can spare the mutton."

Alys was pretty, Lyf saw, with full lips and wide-set blue eyes. Her nut-brown hair hung loose about her shoulders; she must be unwed. She was a good deal larger than most Elythian women. She stood nearly as tall as Kaeldra, and the rich inn fare had rounded her figure and plumped her cheeks. A silver chain was clasped round her wrist, and from it dangled a tiny, silver dove.

"The beasties are happy enough with the brine rats," Yanil said, "and we don't want them gettin' a taste for mutton. No more—do you hear?"

Alys reluctantly nodded.

"Now. This is Lyf, and here"—he set Owyn gently down—"is Owyn." He turned to Lyf. "Alys is sister to the innkeeper here. She'll take good care of you."

Alys smiled. "Are you hungry? I can fetch you a warm pasty or a bit of mutton stew. Cook makes good seedcakes with nutmeg and honey. I can fetch you some."

"Yes!" Owyn said. "I'm hungry!"

Lyf was hungry too, but . . . She turned to Yanil. "Will you stay?"

He shook his head. "I cannot. I'll ferry my load to the potter and then set off for home. I'd best be there when the bounty hunters come."

Lyf felt a wrenching inside her. Alys seemed kind enough, but she didn't *know* Alys. Kaeldra had never spoken of Alys. Lyf had looked to Yanil to take care of her—and now he was leaving.

"I must be off now, Lyfling," he said gently. "You're safe here with Alys. And she'll take you to a place where you'll be safer still."

He took her hand. "You're a good lass, and strong. Kaeldra would be proud."

He squeezed her hand, dropped it, and then slipped out the door.

Harper's Tale

Kaeldra and Jeorg and the harper set off through the night. Nysien took leave of them and soon returned with horses. Stolen horses.

Do not judge them harshly for what I tell next, my ladies. They did not hold with thieving. They had never stolen in their lives. But they set aside their scruples and took the pilfered mounts. Kaeldra was with child, mind you—and nearly crazed with worry over her sister and son.

They rode hard back toward the cave. But Kaeldra was tiring; they stopped at Yanil's steading to rest.

His wife gave them the news: Yanil was gone to Tyneth with Owyn and Lyf and a clutch of baby dragons. All were well—thus far.

Kaeldra wept for joy when she heard it.

They quickly supped, then headed back for Tyneth. Nysien rode ahead, as his mount was swifter than the rest.

Or that was the reason he gave. He did not speak of the secret side trek he would make to tell the Krags.

They would all meet up, he said, at the inn.

And Lyf?

I will come to her, my lady. Never fear.

Chapter 11

Dirty Linen

Alys took clear delight in watching Lyf and Owyn eat. She fetched them platters and baskets and bowls full of food: roast mutton and fowl; seedcakes and oatcakes; a thick savory pottage of lentils and barley and leeks. She set the food on upended casks, placed the lamp there beside, then stacked a heap of grain sacks for Lyf and Owyn to sit down upon. Lyf, seeing that Alys walked with a limp, had offered to help. But Alys tut-tutted her away. Lyf set the egg in a corner; Alys perched her ample frame on a tun of brew and looked on from the shadows as they supped—smiling, asking how each dish suited them, seeming to take as much satisfaction in their repast as if she were eating it herself.

Lyf ate until she was stuffed, until she felt she could roll like a barrel across the floor. She tried not to watch the draclings eat but was drawn to them in morbid fascination. They ripped into the carcass; tore off big, meaty chunks; then gorged themselves, snuffling and snorting, until they had licked the bones clean.

This, too, delighted Alys. Holding up the lamp, she pointed out in whispers how this one's mouth curved in a smile as it ate; how that one pranced across the room, shaking a bloody rib of mutton in its teeth; how another one backed into a post, then spun round snorting smoke as if to do battle with it. She chortled softly when they belched, and giggled at how they waddled about when they were full—sides bulging, bellies dragging on the floor, licking their chops long after the meat was gone.

There was so much meat that even the smallest draclings easily got their fill. Lyf feared that their crunchings and thumpings and shufflings might waken others, but Alys assured her that little could be heard from this room above the stable, for it was well set off from the rest of the inn.

Lyf looked round the shadowed edges of the room, where she could make out the shapes of barrels and crates, baskets and sacks. "Does your brother know about the draclings, then?" she asked.

"Oh dear, no! And he mustn't find out!" Alys's eyes widened in alarm. "He wouldn't understand." She hesitated. "You must think me wicked, going against my own brother's wishes this way."

"N-no," Lyf said.

"Well, he wouldn't hold with it. I don't have to ask—I know. But . . . I was ill when I was young. It was the bone-twisting illness; it set my foot askew. And my mama and da were dead, and my brother was busy with the inn, and there was no one to care for me. And a woman took me in—I hardly knew her. She's gone now—may her soul be at peace—and I never paid her back for what she did. She said she didn't want pay, that she only did what was right. But I *owe*. Do you see that?

My brother doesn't see it; he says I'm addle-witted. But . . ." Alys's high, sweet voice sounded shy. "Do *you* see?"

Lyf nodded. She did.

Yet now, by Alys's way of thinking, *she* would owe, as well.

Alys shrugged and made a rueful face. "But my brother mustn't find out about this—not ever!"

They would leave at dawn, Alys told her. "I always leave at dawn," she said, "when I go to wash the linens. There's a shallow place in the river, outside town, with plenty of smooth rocks for scrubbing. He likes fresh bed linen, my brother does. He says it's pleasing to the fine folk. But I've got a friend of the dove sign. I'll take you to her. I'm thinking. . . . Can you make the draclings stay still in the cart, inside some baskets?"

"I . . . I don't know," Lyf said. "If they were sleeping, yes, but otherwise . . ."

The draclings were not sleeping now. Bellies sagging, they clambered onto piles of sacks and nosed into baskets and crates. Owyn followed them about, brandishing a licked-clean leg bone and mumbling, "Boom! Boom! Boom!"

"I could give them a draught of strong brew," Alys said. "And I have an herb for sleeping. It'll do them no ill. It'll be some time before it takes, but they should be well asleep by dawn."

Lyf considered. "Yes. That would be good, I think." And if the draclings fell asleep earlier, so much the better. Then *she* could sleep as well.

"Lyf! Time to wake!"

Lyf jerked up, fearful at the alarm in the whispered voice. Gray light seeped in through the shuttered window and illuminated Alys before her. Lyf could make out the lumpy heaps of slumbering draclings all around.

So the sleeping herb had held.

Yet something *was* amiss. Noises below. Men's voices, horses clopping and snorting, bridles jingling.

Lyf scooted away from Owyn, careful not to rouse him. She gently removed Kindle from about her neck and unwound Smoak's tail from around her leg, then went to peer out through a crack in the shutters.

Men and horses and dogs milled round in the foggy courtyard below.

"Who—" Lyf began.

"Bounty hunters, here for the wolf's head."

"But how do they know we're *here*?"

"Sh! They *don't* know. It's old rumors they're hearing—the same ones Yanil heard before. They're only guessing. They've no notion you're in town—only nearby. They're going to eat here, plan the day's search."

Alys began pulling out wicker baskets from a nested stack on the floor. "Likely they'll lodge at the inn this night. So I *must* wash the linens now, mustn't I? Mustn't get lice in their fine locks. Not new lice, at any pass. They've brought their own—of that I've no doubt."

Alys hurried off and returned with an armload of linens, then left again for more. Before long the floor was heaped with them.

Owyn still slept—as did the draclings. Now one looked up drowsily, regarded Lyf and Alys with a half-open eye, then tucked its nose back under another dracling's tail. The noises from the courtyard had ceased, except for an occasional snarling scuffle from the hounds below.

"Oh dear," Alys said, peering out through the crack. "Those hounds! I don't like them, I don't! My brother doesn't hold with hounds in the tavern, but they're welcome in the courtyard. As it is, they're right below the stair. If we go out that way, they'll sniff the draclings out—no matter how well hid they are. No matter how deep they're sleeping."

"Should we wait until they're gone?" Lyf asked.

"We could—though that's a risk. They'll be all over town by then. No place'll be free of 'em. They might even think to search the inn. But there's one other thing we might try."

"What's that?"

Alys heaved her shoulders in a deep sigh, shaking her head. "I don't like it," she said. "And neither will you."

"Keep your eyes down, sweeting. Whatever they say to you, don't look up."

Lyf nodded. She pulled the hood of her cloak farther down over her head and, clutching the big wicker basketful of laundry, followed Alys down the corridor to the stairway that led to the tavern.

The dracling was light, and still. Lyf would not have known from the feel of the basket that a dracling was coiled within. But she had put him there herself, and piled the linens atop him. She had put all the draclings into baskets. They had been limp and warm and had peered at her with glazed, heavy-lidded eyes before wrapping their tails about their snouts and resuming their naps. They *liked* dark, close places, Lyf reassured herself.

Now Alys was going down the stairs. Her limp set her gait askew, yet there was an odd, fluid grace to it. Lyf could not see the first step; the basket blocked her view. She scooted her boot along the floor, felt where it dropped off, stepped down with one foot, then the other.

Scoot, step, step.

Scoot, step, step.

Scoot, step, step.

Noise swelled up from the tavern below: men talking and laughing, brew horns clanking. Beyond the edges of her hood now she could see them seated round the trestle tables. Her heart was beating so loud, she felt certain they must hear it. She averted her glance, fixed her mind on finding the steps.

Scoot, step, step.

Scoot, step, step.

Deep within the basket, something moved. <Be still,> she willed, holding her breath. The moving stopped. Likely the dracling had only shifted in its sleep.

They were nearly to the bottom of the stairs. Remembering to keep her eyes downcast, Lyf followed Alys out the front door. The cart, harnessed to a swayback mare, awaited in the street. They were alone—or nearly so. The storefronts stood dark, shrouded in fog. A small herd of goats emerged from the mist, driven through the muddy street by a young boy. But elsewise nothing stirred. Alys took Lyf's basket, hefted it into the cart.

"Well," she said, shrugging. "We've done it. This far, at any pass."

"Were they staring at us?"

"No. I kept fearing they would. But what's to stare at? Two lasses with baskets of dirty linens." She shrugged again.

"And your brother? Did *he* look? Did he wonder he'd never seen me before?"

"No. We go through chambermaids faster than kegs of small ale. This one's off and married, that one's quit for a better wage. He never keeps track of 'em."

There had been no dogs in the tavern—Alys had been right about that. Now they had only to make their way back up the stairs—then do it all over again six more times.

Up in the storeroom at last, Lyf let out a long breath.

"I saw no one look," Alys said. "Did you?"

"No. I kept my eyes downcast all the while."

"Oh, good." Alys giggled. "I forgot. Good lass."

"I'm good too," Owyn said. "I'm hushing! I'm quiet! Aren't I good too?"

"Yes, you're a good, good boy!" Alys said, leaning down to tickle his stomach. Owyn squealed, and Alys hushed him, giggling.

The next trip was easier. Lyf still had to scoot to find the stairs, but she knew the way now. And there were seventeen, exactly seventeen steps. Though her heart still thumped loud in her chest, the men had not taken notice of her before and so, she told herself, likely would not now.

Down seventeen steps. Out the door. Give the basket to Alys. Up seventeen steps. Into the storeroom.

Lyf was feeling bold. Here they were smuggling out the dracIings under the hunters' very noses—and they never knew. They never even guessed.

But in the storeroom after the third trip, Alys turned to her with worried eyes. "Did you see that man? That one that kept staring?"

"No! I was looking down the whole time."

"Well, he did stare," Alys said.

"At me?"

Alys's plump cheeks grew pink. "At *me,* I think. But still... And I fear the sleeping herb is wearing off. My dracling was moving about. Was yours?"

"Only the first one. Only a little."

"Well. Maybe it's nothing. Still, we'd best make haste."

Halfway down the stairs, Lyf felt a tingling in her mind.

Something stirred within the basket. <Be still,> Lyf warned. <Still.> But on the fourteenth stair the basket suddenly lurched. Lyf's foot shot out, missed the step. She lunged forward, falling....

A strong hand gripped her elbow, stayed her fall. "Ho there, milass." Before she had the wits to stop him, a man was taking the basket out of her hands, saying, "I'll deliver this to the buxom wench. How is she called?"

"Alys," Lyf mumbled to the floor, carefully keeping her eyes downcast.

"Alys," he said thoughtfully. "Pretty name—Alys."

Lyf stood still, watching his boots move toward the door, praying the dracling would not shift again. She didn't know whether to stay where she was or follow the hunter or go back up to the storeroom. <Still,> she willed to the dracling. <Stay still.>

She edged toward the door and watched the man walk out into the gray light. She saw Alys startle, and then cover it with a smile. He stood talking to her, drawing nearer and nearer, while Alys, smiling, backed away. Lyf could hear his voice, but the pounding of her heart drowned out his words. Then Alys's voice came loud—too loud—and dismayed: "Oh no, milord, you mustn't trouble—"

"It's no trouble." The man wheeled round and strode toward the door. Lyf started up the stairs as fast as she could without seeming to hurry.

The man's voice sounded below her. "Galum! Bevan! Dwynn! Come help!"

Benches scraping. Heavy, booted footsteps. Deep voices, conferring.

Hurry. Hurry. They mustn't see Owyn. Owyn could *not* keep his green eyes averted; he would give them away.

She reached the landing just as the first footsteps jarred the wooden stairs. Down the hallway. Open the door and shut it behind. "Owyn!" she whispered urgently. "Get in the basket now! The hunters are coming!"

"Why?" Owyn asked. She could hear the rumbling of footsteps: closer, closer. She picked him up, set him down in the empty basket. "We're playing a trick on the hunters," she said desperately. "Hush! Do you hear me? And no drumming. Hush!"

Footsteps on the landing. Lyf grabbed two fistfuls of dirty linen, threw them over Owyn. Two more fistfuls, and her glance snagged on something light in the corner of the room.

The egg. It had come partway out of its carrier.

The door flew open; Lyf looked down and finished filling the basket with linen.

Please don't let them see the egg.

The man who had helped her was counting. "One, two, three, four, five, six. If we each take one, we can be done with it in a single trip."

The draclings were light. But Owyn—he was heavy. If one of them picked up Owyn's basket, he would know something was amiss. Lyf leaned down to claim the basket with Owyn in it. In her mind's eye, the egg glowed like a full moon rising, impossible to miss.

Heavy. Owyn was too heavy. She could never lug him down the steps. She started slowly toward the door because she knew not what else to do, when, "Let me swap with you, now, Lyf," Alys said.

Lyf let out a breath, lowered Owyn to the floor. "Wait," she whispered. She fussed with the linens until the last man had left, then fetched the egg and carrier and slid them deep into the basket. "Here, Owyn. Hold the egg."

The linens moved a bit, and Lyf heard a muffled, "Why?"

"Sh!"

Alys picked up the basket with Owyn and the egg; Lyf snatched up the last remaining basket and followed them down the stairs.

At the cart, one of the men took Lyf's basket and set it within. She started for the seat near Alys, but the man stepped into her path. "My mother taught me," he said, "to say 'Thank you.'"

Lyf looked up, startled. "Thank you!" she said. She ducked her head and scrambled up onto the seat.

"You'll return soon, then?" Alys's admirer was asking her.

She giggled. "Soon enough." She shook the reins. "Git you! Rusty, git!" The cart slowly creaked forward.

Lyf held her breath, waiting for the man to call out, straining to hear his running footsteps. "He saw my eyes," she whispered. She was hot, all-over hot. She wiped her clammy hands on her cloak.

"No, there, sweetie, I'm sure he didn't," Alys assured her.

"Yes. I looked right at him. I didn't mean to. He was blocking my way. He wanted me to thank him, and it startled me."

Alys furrowed her brow. "Oh, dear," she said.

"It was just for a moment. When I was looking at him, I mean."

"Well. Likely he didn't notice." Alys patted Lyf's knee. Lyf could tell she was trying to be comforting. But Alys said nothing for a while after that. She was listening, Lyf thought. As Lyf herself was listening.

Hazy yellow light seeped through the fog from the shop windows. Folk were stirring now. There were other carts about, and people walking. Lyf could hear dogs barking and the clanging of a smithy somewhere beyond.

But no shouting. No following footsteps.

Lyf turned to look back, but Alys laid a restraining hand on her knee. "No. Not yet."

"Can I come out now?" Owyn's voice came from behind.

"No," Lyf said. "We're still playing a trick on the hunters. Just a little while longer—then you may."

Lyf reached out with her mind for the draclings, and felt a waking, a restlessness. <Be still,> she urged.

A questioning in her mind.

<Be still!>

A dog barked—nearer this time. Lyf jumped, started to look back, then remembered herself.

"It's only a little dog," Alys said. "Not like the hunters' hounds."

"Oh." Lyf calmed a bit, but the yapping continued, seemed to grow closer. There was a restlessness, a seething in her mind. The draclings. <Be still,> she told them. <Still.>

And now she heard a second dog, one with a deeper bark. Alys turned back to look. "Oh, dear. It's none of the hunters' dogs," she said, "but it is big. And it's following."

A third dog, a fourth, a whole chorus of dogs joined in. Alys looked back again. "Shoo! Get away, now. Shoo!" She shook the reins. "Faster, Rusty!"

The swayback mare broke into a halfhearted trot, then subsided to a walk. Now dogs beset the cart on all sides, barking, baying, yipping, yapping. The draclings' fears were clattering in Lyf's mind. She turned back to look and saw three narrow heads poking up from the baskets. The little pumpkin-hued dracling huffed out a spray of sparks. <Get down!> Lyf urged, but that only seemed to alarm them. Four more heads popped up, and then Owyn was thrashing up through the linens, peering over the rim of his basket.

"Why are those dogs barking?" he asked.

"They won't harm you," Lyf said. "Get down!"

The cart swerved suddenly; Lyf whirled round to see Rusty toss her head and shy from the pack of barking dogs.

"Shoo!" Alys yelled. "Go away! Shoo!" She snapped the reins feverishly; the cart jerked forward.

People were staring at them now; Lyf could see them coming out of their cottages and shops to gape. "Oh, dear. Oh, dear. Oh, dear." Alys chanted softly, *oh dearing* with every breath. Her gaze was fixed on the road ahead.

There was a bridge, Lyf saw. A narrow plank bridge with a thin wooden rail. The draclings were making a racket in her mind; the dogs were thronging all about in a great, barking horde. The cart lurched in fitful stops and starts as Alys yelled at the dogs and urged the old nag forward. "I'm afraid I'm going to hurt the dogs," she wailed to Lyf. "I'm afraid I'm going to run them down."

<Get down!> Lyf urged the draclings. <Be still!> She heard shouting, turned around to look, and her heart leapt into her throat. Folk running, pursuing. They came clearer now, through the fog: men, women, children, dogs.

A lick of fire: one of the draclings was flaming. Then another and another. Puffs of blue smoke arose from the cart. More fire. One of the baskets was burning.

And now the cart rattled up onto the bridge, but something was dreadfully amiss. They were tilting, they were tipping. . . .

Lyf leaned hard against Alys to keep the cart from overturning, but she couldn't stop it. There was a splintering crash as the railing broke, and they were hurtling through the air—draclings, linens, baskets, all—and the river came rushing up.

Harper's Tale

Tyneth was deserted. Or so they thought at first—Kaeldra and her friends. But, hearing a dull roar, they made their way through empty streets to a throng gathered near a bridge.

Like a fair it was, my ladies—the folk were that thick.

Kaeldra and Jeorg lay low while the harper went for news. And dire enough it was: The innkeeper's sister had fallen into the river—along with two younglings and a passel of draclings.

Chapter 12

The Marsh

The river slammed against her in a jolt of stinging cold. It stopped her breath and, when she gasped for air at last, water sucked up into her nose and filled her throat. Lyf thrashed her arms, trying to drag her head up into the air. Then she was coughing. Gasping. Coughing.

Air.

The bridge arched darkly overhead and then was gone as the current swept her along. Her boots, heavy as iron, dragged her down. Her cloak felt cumbrous as a coat of mail. Lyf pumped her arms and kicked her feet, trying to recall what Jeorg had taught her of swimming.

Owyn. Where was Owyn?

Through the swirling fog, she could see the sleek-dark heads of draclings all about her, bobbing on the stream. A wicker basket grazed her shoulder and went floating past, and then a tangle of linen, bloated with air. She wrenched round to look for Owyn behind her, and a snag was bearing down, a massive stump with a great wide tangle of roots.

"Auntie Lyf!"

She saw him then, head above water, clutching to the roots.

She reached out, grabbed a root, then worked her way hand over hand through the twisted snarl until she came to him. Gladness welled up within her. "Owyn!"

"Auntie Lyf!" he said, and there was a catch in his voice.

"Owyn, are you well? Unharmed?"

He nodded, his eyes so dark and wide and frightened, they seemed to take up half his face. "Did we . . . trick the hunters?" he asked.

Hunters. Lyf craned round to look behind, but could see little beyond the thick pall of fog. The grayness massed darkly to one side—the riverbank, perhaps. She could make out no such border on the other side. The water churned with foam and debris: tree branches, wooden planks, baskets, linens, draclings. Beyond the steady river rush she heard faint, calling voices and the barkings of distant dogs.

Of Alys she saw no sign.

Lyf turned back to Owyn, then her glance caught on a luminous patch of white.

The egg. He held it in its carrier, clasped to his chest.

"Owyn!" she said, stunned. "The egg. How did you . . . ?"

"You told me to hold it."

"Yes, but . . . in the water . . ."

"My da taught it to me, to swim on my back and hold things."

He had *held* it through the fall? She would never have

held it. She would have dropped it with the first freezing shock of river.

Lyf fumbled for the water-soaked carrier, drew its loop over her head. Then Owyn was climbing up through the roots to perch atop the stump. Lyf followed—but more slowly. Her hands had gone numb with cold and would not grip as they ought. Her boots weighed at least ten anchor-weight. Her sopping kirtle got entangled in the roots and between her legs; the egg kept getting in the way. All the while she feared the stump might tip and roll over, but it did not. At last, she dragged herself onto the bole and straddled there behind Owyn. She latched onto him with one hand and grasped a root behind her with the other.

The snag rushed headlong through the fog, jolting over patches of white water, sending sheets of foamy river cascading into their faces. Thank the heavens the stump never rolled—its wide-spreading mass of roots kept the top side ever on top. But it yawed this way and that, and often, jostled by competing eddies, spun round and round again.

Lyf could see draclings—dark splotches in the gray spring flood.

<Come,> she summoned. <Come.> They veered toward the log, gliding like seals through the swollen river. Then they were climbing on, hooking their talons into the wet bark and pulling themselves up among the roots.

The snag rocked but did not tip. The draclings shook themselves, flapping their wings, filling the air with spray. They came nuzzling round Lyf and Owyn—first Skorch, pushing past the others, then the fierce-looking green one, then a pudgy reddish one, and then Smoak, hiccuping, nudging, begging to be scratched.

"I can't scratch you now! Do you want me to fall off?" Lyf said, making her voice sound gruff. Then Kindle was climbing up Lyf's arm and draping herself about Lyf's neck, thrumming wildly. *All* of the draclings were thrumming. And Lyf felt a sudden, sharp surge of unreasonable joy.

She began to count them, but broke off at a sudden shout from behind. Lyf twisted round and saw a dark shape in the fog: a boat. Two boats—no, three—no, four.

All at once something burst inside her head, shattered in blinding splinters of pain. Lyf cried out, pressed her palms into her eyes. Again the pain came. It pulsed against Lyf's skull, dwindled to a dull, aching throb.

What was that?

The draclings crowded round her, mewling. Their fears flooded into her mind.

They must have felt it too.

A hissing sound. Lyf looked up to see that the snag was plowing through reeds—a forest of reeds. It was slowing, stopping. They had fetched up on the riverbank.

The boats. Where were the boats?

Lyf shook her head to clear it, then tried to pull Kindle off her shoulder. The dracling refused to budge, digging her talons into Lyf's flesh. Lyf clambered down from the stump and sank halfway to her knees in muck. *Not* the riverbank. A marsh! She turned round to help Owyn just in time to see him land in splattering mud. The draclings were leaping off the snag all around them, spraying her with scum and mud and water. They milled about her legs; their fears racketed against the inside of her skull.

Lyf pulled Owyn up out of the mud and, pushing the egg to one side, set him on a hip and stumbled through the marsh. She could hear him crying—little gasping sobs. The draclings came splashing after.

Behind came voices—sharp, alarmed. They were nearing.

She struck out blindly away from the river. Her neck ached from lugging Kindle and the egg. Her dripping cloak and kirtle dragged her down. Mud pulled hard at her boots. *Please,* she thought, *don't let it be a suck-bog.* One of the draclings got entangled in her legs; she tripped, fell, pulled herself to her feet. She tried to keep to the thickest clusters of marsh grass, hoping soon to feel solid ground beneath her. But the marsh was honeycombed with rivulets and streams, and mist clung thick and opaque to the ground. Lyf could not see clearly where she was putting her feet, and once plunged chest-deep into water. When she found the shallows again, she set down Owyn and resettled Kindle and the egg carrier about her chafing neck. Holding tight to Owyn's hand, she skirted the edges of reedy thickets, trying to find a way through. Then she pushed aside a curtain of mallow grass and there was a mound of dry, hummocky land, where the ground did not squish underfoot.

Lyf and Owyn slumped down on the reeds. The draclings came thrumming about, butted their heads at the egg, nuzzled her neck. Kindle slid down from her shoulders to her lap. Still frightened they were—Lyf could feel it—though not so strongly as before. "Sh!" she said. "Let me listen!"

The reeds around them rose eerily from the mist; she could see nothing beyond. But she heard voices and splashing sounds. The draclings seemed to sense the need for caution; they sat still, cocking their narrow heads to one side as if listening. The voices seemed to come from all directions: approached, receded, approached. Lyf ached to move, to run, to flee—but forced herself to stay. If she could hear them moving, they could hear *her* moving. Especially with the draclings. A holt cat's prey, she knew, was safe until it stirred; the holt cat could not see it else.

Now *they* were the prey.

The voices grew fainter. The draclings visibly calmed. Some of them trod round and round, trampling down the reeds before settling down. Others began licking their claws to clean them.

"Are they gone?" Owyn whispered.

Lyf shook her head *no*. She could still hear voices, far off. She could not tell where they came from—whether they were returning to the river or still searching. In fact, she was not certain any longer which way the river lay.

She strained her ears through the marsh sounds—the constant, high chirpings of frogs, a faint rustling of reeds, the musical *ploink* of something falling into the water. She breathed in the rich smell of marsh rot, overlaid by the fragrance of flowers and new, green, growing things, overlaid by the smell of wet wool.

"I'm cold," Owyn said. He was shivering, Lyf saw. His throat-ill would come back.

Only then did she realize that she was shivering too. Her kirtle clung to her back and shoulders, heavy and clammy and chill. She wrung out her braid and the hood of her cloak; it didn't help.

"Lie down," she said to Owyn.

"Why?"

Lyf gave him a look; he obeyed. Gently, she pushed Kindle off her lap. She found Smoak among the welter of draclings and pulled him atop Owyn. The dracling was limp, sleepy, compliant. Owyn shivered, curled up tighter. Smoak hiccuped once, thrummed, settled in.

"Is that better?"

"Um," Owyn said. "He's warm!"

Lyf tried to sort out whole draclings from the tangle of heads and backs and tails. *Nine*. That couldn't be. She counted again. Eleven. Better. But there had been thirteen! She called silently into the mist, <Come!> but heard nothing, felt nothing. Then she remembered the twin bursts of pain in her head.

Might they . . . have been killed?

<Come,> Lyf called. <Come!>

The draclings stretched up, cocked their heads, listening.

But there was nothing.

Well, perhaps they are only lost, Lyf thought. But she could not forget that blinding-bright pain.

The draclings snuggled in again. Kindle crept toward Lyf, clambered up and draped herself about Lyf's neck. Thank the heavens she was so light. Warmth seeped through Lyf's sodden cloak, flowed deep into her neck and shoulders and back. She scratched the little one's floppy crest. Kindle lifted her chin; Lyf scratched in the hollow beneath her jaw. The dracling began to thrum, her throat vibrating like the low string on a harp.

Lyf surveyed the other draclings, trying to recall which ones were missing. Skorch sat in the middle of the heap, looking round alertly. Smoak lay atop of Owyn, hiccuping softly into his ear. Skorch and Smoak and Kindle were the only names Lyf knew. The others had not offered their names, and she had not pressed. A dragon's name was a rare gift, Kaeldra had told her, and must be freely given.

Still, Lyf recognized the others: the fierce-looking female, with her high-arching eye ridges; the big, pudgy reddish one.

Where was the clumsy one who had backed into the post? No—wait. There she was, burrowed way down deep in the pile. But . . . where were Kindle's siblings? The one the color of green apples, who liked to nibble Lyf's fingers? The feisty pumpkin-colored one who was always spitting sparks? Lyf scanned the mound of draclings but could find no trace of them.

She remembered how, when she had taken care to feed them at Yanil's cottage, they had not wanted her to leave. They had *trusted* her.

Perhaps they are there beneath the others, Lyf told herself. Or hiding somewhere in the marsh. But a heaviness hung about her heart.

She stroked Kindle's head, and the tattered skin came sloughing off—almost transparent, like a snake's skin when it sheds. She combed Kindle all over with her fingers, collected stray shreds of skin and tucked them into her sash. The knobs on Kindle's shoulders were . . . blooming. Their hard, outer husks sloughed off in Lyf's hands, revealing shimmery wing-stuff, curled tight but unfurling at the edges like petals bursting from the bud. Lyf hoped the little dracling had not left a trail of shedding skin all throughout the marsh. And the others . . .

Her heart constricted.

My fault.

Owyn stirred and moaned. The draclings made little snoring sounds; thin wisps of smoke twined up from their snouts and blended with the fog. But Lyf could not think of sleep. She was drawn tauter than a warp thread on a new-strung loom. She tried to plan what they would do next, but her mind kept blinking out flashes of things she did not want to see: of Kaeldra's capture, of the two little draclings, of Alys. She wondered what had befallen Alys. Had she plunged into the river and drowned? Had the hunters seized her? Hurt her?

No. Lyf brushed the thought aside.

No.

She crouched in the mist, feeling her bloodbeat subside. The men's voices sounded faintly, far away. She could see nothing—nothing save for Owyn and the pile of sleeping draclings—and beyond, the tips of reeds and encircling fog. Owyn slept; Smoak rode gently up and down on his chest, in rhythm with Owyn's breathing.

They were alone.

They could not go home—nor to Yanil, nor to Alys. Kaeldra and Jeorg were captives, and Lyf had no means of finding Alys's friend.

There was no one in the whole wide world to take care of them now.

Harper's Tale

Not a single boat was to be had in all of Tyneth. The harper begged, bargained, lied, cajoled, offered to buy. But all were on the river, chasing draclings.

CHAPTER 13

Bird Kenning

As the day wore on, the fog grew thin and then burned off entirely. Lyf did not dare venture from the reed-screened hummock where they lay, for fear they would be seen. The voices came more rarely now, and yet come they did, rising over the rustling of reeds and the sluggish plash of marshy water, rising from this direction and then that—sometimes faintly, sometimes so clear and loud that Lyf clenched with fear and sent out a fearful <Hush hush hush hush hush!> to the sleeping draclings.

Sunlight streamed in shafts through the veil of reeds. It sent up clouds of steam from Lyf's sodden gown, warming her through. It played across Owyn's freckled face and struck sparks of shimmering light off the draclings' scales. Beneath the fragrance of blossoms and tender green shoots swelled the marshy reek of decay.

Owyn woke, foraged round for mallow grass, and nibbled off the feathery young tops. Lyf found a cluster of purple-blooming marshwort; she tugged up the stalks and shared the roots with Owyn. "Hush," she told him, when he asked when they would leave. "The searchers are still about."

"But when will we find Mama?" he insisted.

"Soon," she said, having no idea when *soon* would come—if ever.

Owyn drowsed again, nestled in with the heap of draclings. They slumbered as well, twitching their tails from time to time at the stinging bugs and, perhaps disturbed by some dragonish dream, snorting out tendrils of bluish smoke. Lyf silently called to the little ones, now gone.

Nothing.

A wave of aching engulfed her.

Still, it was good that the other draclings slept, for she had nothing to feed them. Lyf wondered if Alys's potion still held or if they always slept so much.

Alys.

Lyf let herself think of Alys—truly *think* of her—for the first time since falling into the river.

Had she drowned? But no. Surely she had not. Surely she had gone safe to dry land.

But what then? The hunters knew by now that she had smuggled draclings out of the inn—as did her brother. What would they do to her? How would her life be now?

She had *owed*, Alys said, but had she owed this much?

Would I *have risked my life,* Lyf wondered, *if I had not been forced to?*

No. She knew she would not have. She would have been too fearful for herself.

And now Alys was . . . wherever she was. And Lyf and the draclings were alone.

What should they do now?

If only Lyf had asked *where* Alys's friend lived. But she hadn't. She didn't know.

There was but one frail thread to go on. Kaeldra had spoken of a last remaining mother dragon, in a cave far to the north. "Where the land meets the Northern Sea," she had said.

But how far that was, Lyf did not know. Nor *where*, exactly. *Where the land meets the Northern Sea* was not much to go by.

Still, it was all they had.

A damselfly went humming past, a shimmer of blue. Nearby, a butterfly sunned itself drunkenly on a clump of steeple-brush blooms. Their perfume lay thick and sweet in the air.

How might she find it? Lyf wondered. That dragon cave. How?

Bloodflies gathered in drowsy, buzzing clouds, raising welts on Lyf's hands and neck. Her head began to ache. Tired. She was tired. Her thoughts came muzzy, confused. She couldn't think.

She let her gaze linger on the slow movement of breath in the draclings' sides, on the rise and fall of Owyn's belly. She leaned back, felt the egg humming against her. The air droned, warm and lulling. . . .

"Auntie Lyf!"

She opened her eyes.

"Auntie Lyf, look!"

A jolt of terror shot through her. She sat up fast, dumping Kindle off. She scanned the marsh for the hunters, but she could not see far. A chill mist had stolen in through the reeds, clinging to earth and water. She must have slept through the better part of the day.

"Look *there,*" Owyn said.

Lyf gazed up to where he pointed—and then she saw.

The draclings were floating.

She counted six of them—no, seven—no, eight. They *hovered* in the mist, just above the reeds.

Kaeldra had told her of this, that draclings floated in their sleep. Lyf wondered why she had never seen them floating before. She thought back to the many times she had been with them as they slept: in the stump, at Yanil's cottage, in Yanil's cart, at the inn. Had they been floating all along . . . while *she* was sleeping?

<Come down!> Lyf commanded. <Down!>

They made no move to obey, but bobbled gently, rising slowly, like wyffel fluff on the air. One more dracling drifted up from among the ghostly reeds, and then another.

Ten. All but Kindle.

A sudden lick of blue flame; one of the draclings sank down. A puff of bluish smoke mingled with the mist.

Lyf reached out to touch the draclings' minds. Silence.

They *were* sleeping.

Another burst of flame; a second dracling drifted lower, then began again to rise. Lyf crept cautiously to her feet, not knowing quite what to do. A sea of shoulder-high reeds hemmed them in for as far as she could see. She could not tell how far the marsh stretched, for it was blurred in all directions by fog. She could not see the river they had come from. Higher up, the fog thinned and Lyf caught glimpses of blue sky. A blue trail of smoke twisted up from where the last dracling had flamed, wafting beyond the mist into clear air.

"How long have they been doing this?" Lyf asked.

"I don't know," Owyn said. "They were doing it when I woke."

"If the hunters are still about, they'll find us by the smoke!"

Before, there had been only the wispiest breaths of smoke. But this flaming . . .

Perhaps they had not been floating and flaming for long, Lyf hoped.

"Draclings, come down!" Owyn shouted.

Three draclings coughed out flame in startlement; two of them plummeted into the reeds at Lyf's feet. One, farther afield, plunged into the water with a splash.

"Hush, Owyn! The searchers might still be near."

"Why?" Owyn asked.

"Because they want to kill the draclings."

"Why?"

Lyf sighed. Was this a serious *why* or just a ploy to keep her talking? At any pass, it was too tangled—and too gruesome—to explain. "Just because, Owyn. Just because."

Silently she pleaded, coaxed, *commanded* the remaining draclings to come down, but they either would not or *could* not. Awake now, they peered curiously down at her with green, slotted eyes. Their bodies seemed rounder than before. Bloated. Their wings, half-extended, were still.

The one named Skorch floated just above Lyf's head. If he kept on rising he would soon drift beyond her grasp. She stood on tiptoe and took hold of the dracling's leg. His wings gave a sudden, jerky flutter, but he did not otherwise protest. Gently, Lyf pulled him down until she could set her hands on his back between his wings and push. It was not difficult—like pushing a big chunk of floating cork down through water. When he rested on the ground, Lyf drew in a deep breath, wiped the sweat from her hands. She brought down another dracling in this way, then a third. They did not seem to mind, but by the time the third one was down, Skorch had bobbled up again and floated knee-high. Lyf started to push him down again, but he fluttered his wings and squirted forward, eluding her.

"You little guttersharp," she muttered, lunging at him. She caught him and set him on the ground, less gently than before.

<Stay,> she said.

But now the other draclings had discovered the game, and they did not want to abandon it. Lyf stumbled across the hummock after them, trying to avoid stepping on the ones on the ground. Owyn began to laugh. "It's not funny!" she snapped. "Help me!" Owyn gleefully lunged after the draclings, but even the ones he wrestled to the ground soon rose again.

Stupid things! She was trying to save them; didn't they understand? She should leave them here to be discovered—she *should*.

"Lie down!" she ordered Owyn, and when he did, she plucked a dracling out of the air and stuffed it under his legs. Then she packed one beneath each of his arms. Owyn giggled as the draclings buoyed him up, arms and legs and back, until only his seat touched the ground. Then the one beneath his legs wriggled out from under and floated into the air. "Hold him!" Lyf said, but it was too late.

This ploy wasn't going to serve; Lyf could see that now.

Skorch drifted up before her. Teasing her?

"Do you want them to catch you?" Lyf asked. "The hunters? The soldiers?" How could she make them see?

Lyf made a picture in her mind of the boats that had

come after them in the fog. She recalled the pain, the pain in her head.

Skorch spat out flame, alit with a thud at her feet.

Fear. Lyf could feel his fear. She could feel it pouring out to the other draclings, infecting them.

Flame!

Flame!

Flame!

Within moments, they were all on the ground.

"Well," Lyf said. "Well." She heaved out a breath, relieved.

But ghostly spiderwebs of smoke wafted up from where the flaming had been, signaling their whereabouts for all to see.

They would have to leave—and now.

But where? They had no destination—only a feeble hope.

North. All hope lay to the north.

They set off through the marsh. At first, the westering sun hung low above the mist, staining it the color of muskmelon flesh. But the sun was sinking and the mist was rising; before long the mist engulfed them completely and the sun was but a smoky orange smudge. Still, Lyf could reckon north by it; she doggedly bore that way. Though it was not easy, heading north. Ever and again she had to veer off course to skirt the edges of deep pools or patches of ominous-looking mud.

And ever she worried about hunters.

Owyn had revived and matched her pace, beating the air with two sticks he had found and making soft-voiced *booms*. The draclings romped through the marsh, vanishing into the mist and then reappearing suddenly beside her. They flung themselves into the deepest pools and channels and shook off water in sheets when they came to dry ground. Some of them began to play at flying. At first Lyf forbade them, fearing that they might be seen. They heeded her better now, or perhaps it was Skorch whom they minded. But as the mist grew thicker, and even Skorch began to fly, Lyf let it go. For a long while, she had had neither sight nor sound of hunters. Surely none would see.

The draclings floated up into the air, wobbling, reeling side to side, pumping their frail-looking wings. Sometimes they crashed through the reeds to land; sometimes they belched out flame and plummeted to the ground. Lyf fretted that they might set something afire—and yet everything was damp. Too damp, surely, to burn.

Lyf fretted too that the draclings would begin plaguing her with their *hungries*. But that fear was soon put to rest. She noticed at times that they sat stone still, gazing intently at something she could not see in the water. Then they would plunge in headfirst and come up chomping. Chomping . . . what, Lyf wondered? But then she marked a frog's kicking leg before it disappeared between the curve of needle-sharp teeth.

Frogs must be slower than twitchmice.

And still, neither sight nor sound of hunters. In time, this gave Lyf comfort. Foolish comfort, she knew, for the mist now eddied so thickly about that she could *not* have seen them, were they only as far away as a cottage is wide. The smudge of sun had faded, and yet she thought she could remember where it had been.

They slogged through the mire, keeping to the clumps of reeds as often as they might, but forced at times to wade through knee-high water, thigh-high water. The reek of marsh rot grew stronger now, drowning out the fragrance of flowers. Reeds slashed at Lyf's and Owyn's hands and necks and faces, leaving fine traceries of blood. Lyf's kirtle grew sodden and draggled; the egg hung heavier with every step. Kindle rode upon her shoulders and, though her neck was cramping up, Lyf couldn't dislodge her, lest the dracling be lost, like her siblings.

Now Owyn lagged behind no matter how often Lyf stopped to wait for him. From time to time he sat down in the mud, refusing to go on. Then Lyf would haul him up and balance the solid mass of him on one hip, turning her head so that he could not see the tears that streaked her face. Her eyes and back and legs and arms and hands all ached. Her feet grew cold and numb—all but the places where the blisters had popped. These burned like fire. Her stomach gnawed painfully, whether only from hunger or from the bitter mallows as well Lyf did not know or care. She was weary to the bone.

Darkness thickened around them, seeming to seep up from the water into the reeds. Yet it was not nearly so dark as in the forest. A swollen half-moon floated in the mist, infusing it with a milky radiance.

How wide *was* this marsh? Surely they would come to the end of it soon!

The chirp of frogs filled the night, broken at times by ominous swishes and splashes and stretches of unfathomable silence. The bloodflies had gone, but Lyf soon discovered a worse pestilence. When they trudged up out of the muck to a dry hummock, Lyf saw a dark blob on Owyn's neck.

A leech.

Swallowing a scream, she plucked it off and flung it down. Owyn cried out, moving his hand to touch the trickle of blood where the leech had been. Another leech, clinging to his wrist. She pulled it off, then saw the leech on her own arm. She did scream then, but before she could rip it off, Skorch was there, was licking her arm with a long, forked tongue, and the leech was gone. Lyf screamed again, waving him away, then stood watching him chew, watching him gulp and lick his chops.

The draclings gathered about them. Lyf felt them nuzzling at the backs of her legs, snuffling at her hands. Owyn slumped down on the hummock and let them nuzzle him all over. Lyf hesitated, then sat down and gave herself over to the draclings' leech pickings, her stomach knotted in revulsion.

She couldn't abide this! They had to get out of this odious swamp! She couldn't stay here overnight. *Couldn't.*

There was a sudden rattling in the reeds before her: a heron, mounting up through the fog. She almost threw her kenning out to meet it, then held back.

It was perilous—too perilous.

Owyn crawled into her lap, crowding out two draclings. He clung to her, shaking with sobs. Tears plowed through furrows in the grime on his face.

More rattling: another heron.

She would chance it, this once.

"I'm going to ken with that bird," she murmured to Owyn, not knowing if he would understand. "Stay here. Don't go away."

She threw her thoughts up to the heron. The birdness closed in around her; the ground tipped and swayed below. She could hear fish breathing under water. She could smell snakes and moths and grubs. She winged up through the thinning mists and came out into a clear, dark sky, speckled with stars. There were hills ahead, *dry* hills. There were . . .

A deep, fast pulsing of blood; it merged with her own, and her troubles dropped away behind.

Harper's Tale

Nysien had tidings.

The harper met up with him at dusk that day. The younglings were safe, Nysien said. He had it from an honest fisherman that a friend had taken them all downriver—Lyf, Owyn, and the draclings. They were journeying, Nysien said, to the cave of the last mother dragon.

And—by sheerest luck—Nysien had procured a boat. They could follow along the route Lyf had taken.

That Nysien!

Wasn't he a marvel, my ladies?

Perhaps *too* much of one, was what Jeorg and the harper wondered. But Kaeldra, full of new hope, could not bear even to think it.

Chapter 14

Lunedweth

The smell brought her up—a sharp, acrid stench that sent tears springing into her eyes. From somewhere above came a faint, soft, tinkly sound. Lyf opened her eyes. Overhead, the sun and moon and stars were spinning, shimmering, chiming. Glints of colorful light swam before her. She heard voices, faraway voices, becoming brighter and brighter, as if she were swimming up toward them from the bottom of a clear, dark lake.

Lyf closed her eyes and sank down again into the cool darkness, away from the voices.

That smell again! Familiar, somehow. And something else, something niggling at the edges of her mind. Something poking at her sides.

She opened her eyes and saw them, the draclings, thronging about her. They shoved their noses against her, snorted out smoke.

Lyf tried to sit up, but the movement sent a stab of pain through her head, made it feel heavy and wobbly and dizzy. She lay back down, and now Owyn was there with the draclings above her, blotting out some of the stars. He was saying something. "Auntie Lyf," he was saying. "Wake up, Auntie Lyf." His eyes were red; he had been crying. And now she heard another voice, a woman's voice, a voice she did not know.

"She's with us again," the voice said. "'Twas the moon-phase incantation brought her back—or mayhap the smelling bitters."

Smelling bitters. *That* was the stench.

Owyn moved away, and a sudden wave of uneasiness engulfed Lyf. Something fearsome. Something she must remember. She forced herself to focus, to come up out of the deep place where she had been and fix her attention on this other place, this place with Owyn and the draclings.

There was a small, thatched roof above her head—it still was spinning—and yet the sun and moon and stars shivered below it. How could that be? But no—they were not truly the sun and moon and stars, Lyf saw now, but only baubles made of tin and crystal, dangling by threads from the rafters, sending little patchy rainbows trembling across the walls.

And now the draclings were clambering up onto her stomach, sitting on her chest. The one called Smoak had the hiccups. The one called Skorch huffed a cloud of smoke into her face. Lyf sat up, coughing, and the draclings tumbled to the floor.

She saw them then, the others, standing a little way back: a dark-haired boy of about her own age, and a woman most strange—pale-skinned with purplish, hennaed hair loose and wild down to her waist.

The fear came surging back. Lyf looked frantically round for some way to hide the draclings, but it was too late. They were plain to view; there was no hiding them.

The woman was talking. Something about friends. Something about the draclings.

A strange lightness about her neck. Lyf felt for the egg. Gone.

"It looked cumbrous. I put it there," the woman said, pointing to where the bulging egg sack nestled in a heap of straw on the floor. Her fingers were long and bony, with nails stained as purple as her hair. A jumble of silvery hoops and chains jangled on her arm. Lyf tried to read her face—a long, lean, windburned face with dark-brown, penetrating eyes. A face no longer youthful, but not yet old.

She couldn't read it. Lyf looked away and scanned the room, which seemed to have stopped spinning at last. A hut it was, where fantastical objects bided side by side with ordinary ones. Among the dangling ornaments hung strings of half-waxed candlewicks and a side of mutton blackening in the smoke from the hearth. Sunlight streamed in through the shutters and smokehole, illuminating a three-legged iron kettle over the fire. Something bubbled within; it smelled burnt. There were two rickety stools and, on the far wall from the egg sack, a straw pallet. Open books were strewn about a trestle table and surrounded by all manner of candlesticks—wood and clay and iron. Drying on a rack near the fire were two tattered lengths of wool and one of linen. Lyf looked quickly down at the kirtle she wore. Not her own. Hers must be on the rack along with her shift and the cloak Kaeldra had lent her.

The draclings came crowding round again, sniffing her, nudging at her hands, begging to be scratched. Absently she stroked them, scratched their heads and necks and chins. Kindle climbed up onto her shoulders. Owyn snuggled in beside her.

"How are you faring?" the woman asked. "You were somewhere far away."

"The marsh," Lyf said, her voice rusty from not having spoken. She recalled the marsh now—and the leeches. Her head still ached as if someone had beat a gong inside it and the reverberations wouldn't stop.

"Aye, we're all in a marsh, lass, in a manner of speaking. But you, you were in another place entire. In the soul of a bird, I'm guessing, from what the lad's been saying. I didn't think I could bring you back."

The heron. Lyf remembered now. She had gone with the heron to find a way out of the marsh. But, "What is this place?" she demanded. "Who are you?"

The woman chuckled. "You *are* faring better now—that's plain to see. The humors are in their proper balance, and the planets are harmonious. Anyway," she added, "you've slept it off."

The woman motioned toward the table. Her bracelets tinkled on her wrist. "Come, lass. I'll get you some stew."

Stew. All at once, Lyf felt famished. She rose shakily to her feet; her legs were weak as twigs. The woman plucked Kindle from Lyf's shoulders, then pushed aside the clutter of books and candlesticks to clear a place at the table. She ladled out a bowl of greeny-brown stew and set it down before Lyf. It was the worst-tasting stew she had ever eaten—bitter and burnt and strange. Lyf wondered if it were tainted. But she was famished, and the stew, once down, felt warm and satisfying.

The draclings thrummed and rubbed against Lyf's legs. They must have been fed, and recently, or they would have been plaguing her with their *hungries.*

And yet Lyf still did not know who this woman was, nor why she was helping them. Nor if she were truly helping, or only preparing to betray them.

"I am called Lunedweth," the woman replied, seeming to guess her thoughts. "And this here lad is my own dear cousin's son, Spens. He found you in the marsh."

Spens smiled and ducked his head. He was lean and tanned, with smokey-gray eyes at once curious and shy. Lyf liked the look of him.

As Lyf ate, Lunedweth, aided by Owyn and Spens, related all that had passed while she was entranced within the bird. Spens had been on his way to Lunedweth, whom he stayed with from time to time, helping with odd chores. His parents had died; he lived with his uncle and aunt in the village of Merdoc. Spens had heard crying in the marsh and had followed the sound until he came upon Owyn and Lyf and the draclings. He had heard tell of draclings, so he was not so astounded as he might have been, though, "I *was* afeared," he admitted. Somehow, he had lifted Lyf into his boat, and Owyn after, and had taken them to Lunedweth.

Lyf was chagrined to think how this boy had lifted her bodily into his boat. But, "What of the draclings?" she asked. "How did *they* come here?"

"They wouldn't let you out of their sight," Spens said. "I thought they would flame at me, just touching you, just coming near you. But the lad spoke to them, and they didn't harm me. They snorted out smoke, though, and lashed their tails. And they followed close behind you all the while."

"First they flew away," Owyn said. "They were chasing after that bird. But I called them, and back they came. After the bird was gone."

"They were chasing . . . the heron?" Lyf asked.

"Aye. They were following where you went."

Lyf looked at him, wondering. *How did you know they were chasing the heron?* she almost asked. For it had been dark; the heron would soon have vanished. And how much did Owyn know about bird kenning? She had never spoken to him of it, other than to say she was going to do it. But . . . Lyf believed what he said. There was some kind of . . . knowing . . . that passed between Owyn and the draclings. How had he put it? It *sparkles,* he had said.

"You were in deep—so you were," Lunedweth said. "I couldn't tell if I might fetch you back. A heron was it, you said?"

Lyf hesitated, then nodded.

"And done this before, have you?"

How much should she tell? Lyf didn't know.

"I *needed* to . . . to find our way out of the marsh," she said at last.

"How many times?" Lundeweth demanded. "How many times have you done this?"

Lyf shrugged.

"Once only? *Twice?*"

There had been two other times of going down deep: That once when she was little, and then when the message dove came. Lyf nodded, grudgingly.

"This was your *third* time?"

Lyf looked away. Lunedweth wasn't her mama. She had no business chiding her.

"Small wonder I had such a tribulation pulling you out!" Lunedweth exploded. "The third time! Don't you know that when you go way deep down within the soul of a thing, you might never come back? Few enough folk there have been who ever could do it, and we know of them only from the old tales. There was the one trapped within a swan, never to return. She stayed alive—but barely—until the swan met its death. Then she died too. And that was but her second time kenning. And she was a powerful sorceress! They'll put me in the books for fetching you out—so they will!

"But, lass!" Lunedweth's face grew grave. "It'll suck the spirit from you, this kenning. It takes you deeper each time you go, until you forget who you are, where you come from . . . *what* you are. Only the hardiest souls, grown strong by the bearing of great sacrifice, can hope to cling to a knowing of themselves. And you've lived far too little of life for that. And you look far too soft, if you'll pardon me saying.

"And once this life's forgot, there's no return. Even with me to bring you out. Do you understand me, lass? You would be gone!"

Lyf nodded, frightened. She had never—quite—believed in the danger of bird kenning. She had *touched* their minds so often. But she recalled how she had felt this time when she had awakened. As if she had come up from a great depth. The dizziness, the feeling that she had been drained of life. Much worse than the time before. She *still* felt weak from it, and muzzy. If Lunedweth hadn't brought her out . . .

She would not think of that. Still, she knew this: She would never ken with a bird again!

But this Lunedweth . . . Might she be one of the dove sign? Lyf looked about the hut, searching for something in the shape of a dove. She scanned the walls, the doors, the candlesticks, the hanging ornaments, Lunedweth's clutter of tinkling bracelets. There were all manner of circles and stars, crescents and crosses—but not a dove among them. Not *one*. True, Lyf hadn't seen the lintel. Though not all of the dove sign carved their lintels. She daren't *ask* about the dove sign—that was too perilous. But ... A test. She needed a test.

"Did you feed the draclings brine rats?" she asked.

"Brine rats?" Lunedweth looked perplexed. Out of the corner of her eye, Lyf saw Spens give a start.

"The draclings aren't hungry anymore," Lyf said. "Did you feed them brine rats?"

"No, I fed them a batch of dried toads I keep about me for spells. Every last one they ate! A year's worth of spell toads—gone in a trice! But brine rats ... What are brine rats, pray tell? They're not good for removing warts and corns, now, are they?"

"Corns? No. Or ... I don't think so." Lyf stopped, confused. "Well, then why are you doing this? Helping us? Feeding us?"

Now Lunedweth looked perplexed. "Why? Because you were needin' it, lass."

Lyf took a chance. "But the Krags *are* looking for us, you know. If they found you protecting us, you'd suffer for it."

Lunedweth laughed. "So threaten me something new! Why do you think I live out here on this cursed crannog? I once worked a spell on a Kragish lord to remove a corn from his toe. Alas, his humors were not in harmony and the cycles were out of kilter. In short, his toe fell off. He harried me out of town, and I've not laid eyes on another cogging Krag ever since."

"But . . ." Lyf, desperate, tried again. "Did they find your doves?"

"Doves? What are you prating of, lass? Doves! Brine rats! Are you wildered in your wits?"

She truly did not understand, Lyf saw. "It's only . . . I'm looking for someone . . . of the dove sign."

"The dove sign!" Lunedweth turned to Spens, who had suddenly found a candlestick that needed polishing. "Do you know her meaning, Spens?"

"No," he mumbled, scrubbing hard, not looking up.

Lunedweth stared at him for a time, then leveled her gaze at Lyf. "I'll tell you this, lass—I'll tell you true. I'm no friend to the Krags, and I'd be pleased to do anything to be thwartin' their plans. But that's not the reason I'm feedin' and shelterin' the lot of you. You were needin' help, so I gave it. It's that simple. If you can't understand that, then I pity you—so I do."

Harper's Tale

Why do some folk shut their doors upon the misery of their neighbors, while other folk open them wide?

'Tis a matter the sages have long debated, my lords and ladies. Yet the puzzle remains.

Kaeldra grew ill upon the river, and yet no one they met along the way, seeing the green in her eyes, would tend to her.

These were not evil folk, my ladies. They were only more fearful for the distant dangers to themselves than for the certain dangers to others.

Can you fault them for that?

Can you say in truth that *you* have never acted so?

What's that you say? Get on with the tale?

Very well, my lord (though a draught of brew would surely soothe my poor, parched throat).

On with the tale: With many a rousing adventure, Kaeldra and her friends made their way downriver to a fisherman in the village of Merdoc.

There, my lord. Is that *on with it* enough?

Chapter 15

The Hatching

Late that day there came a change in the weather. Wind gusts rattled fitfully at the shutters; the shafts of filtered sunlight suddenly paled, and then vanished altogether.

Lunedweth lighted an ancient oil lamp, which smoked and guttered in the invisible eddies that slipped in through shutters and doors.

The hut remained dark as a cave.

Lyf washed her face and neck and arms in a bucket of water, then drew on her dry shift and kirtle. Owyn's garments were dry as well, and his throat-ill had not returned.

Spens went outside with Lunedweth to stake down his boat, then they herded the goat within. The draclings rushed at it, spitting out sparks; the goat bleated and lowered its head. But Spens spoke softly to the goat, and Lunedweth gave up a barrelful of dried newts to distract the draclings. They abided in an uneasy peace.

Not trusting the draclings with the chickens, Lunedweth did not take the birds inside, but tied down their coop without.

While the draclings drowsed and Owyn drummed with a spoon on a tin cup that Lunedweth had lent him, Lyf ventured out too, glancing up at the lintel as she went.

No dove. She had known it would not be there, but she couldn't help looking.

Wind whipped her hair about her face and churned in the rushes, turning their silvery undersides out, patterning the marsh with shifting whorls and ripples for as far as Lyf could see. She surveyed for the first time the crannog on which the hut sat. It was a crude heap of slaggy stone, encrusted with a veneer of soil too thin for even the meanest of gardens. The folk before the road builders, Lunedweth had explained, had built many such islands—for what purpose no one knew. "Though I'll wager," she said, "their purpose and mine are the same: the earth energies are strong here. There's a flux in the streams of power. Anyway," she added, "few enemies care to traverse a marsh."

Soon Lyf would have to traverse it again, go searching for this cave to the north where the land met the sea. But not today. She was yet too weak from the kenning, and the sky was too ominous. To the west it was a strange, greeny color, nearly overrun with skudding clouds.

Lunedweth came to stand beside her. "The last time I saw the sky that color, there was a whirlwind that sucked the water out of the marsh and set it down in another place," she said.

"And your hut . . . yet stood?" Lyf asked.

"The better part of it."

Inside, Lunedweth piled up a heap of straw for Lyf and Owyn to sleep on and handed them each a sheepskin. They retired early; the draclings soon gathered about them. Lyf was spent. She felt all of the strength drain out of her and seep down through the floor. And yet she slept but fitfully, half-awakened from time to time by the wind racketing at the shutters and whuffling in the thatch.

Sometime later she came full awake. There was a pelting of rain on thatch—hard rain—and a gusting of wind. The suns and moons and stars chimed gently above, and the pages of books rustled. One of the shutters had come loose and now banged against the wall.

But that wasn't what had wakened her. She knew that wasn't it.

In the light of the glowing embers, Lyf made out the shapes of Owyn and the draclings slumbering round her. She searched for Lunedweth and Spens, and found them asleep in their separate corners. But there was something, something else. . . .

And then she heard it—another sound. It was a soft thumping that seemed to come from *within* the cottage.

Lyf scanned the dark room—the dangling stars, the candlesticks, the opened books, the kettle.

There. Again. Down low. Lyf turned to look where the sound had come from, but saw only the egg sack on the floor by the wall. As she watched, the sack moved, clunked softly against the wall.

It was the egg.

A shiver jolted up Lyf's spine, tingled at the base of her scalp.

It was hatching.

What should she do?

Lyf pushed back the sheepskin, tiptoed through the mass of sleeping draclings, and knelt down on the floor. She drew back the carrier, touched the egg. It was warm—much warmer than before. The humming was loud now—very loud.

Agitation. She could feel an agitation. She could feel a *consciousness*. Lyf picked up the egg, drew it into her lap. The humming coursed all through her, throbbed down through her bones to her fingertips, to her toetips.

The egg lurched in her hands. She held it gently, firmly, until she was sure that it had stopped. Then she moved her hands all around its surface. She felt the smoothness of the egg, the tiny grooves, and there . . . a crack.

"It's time, then, is it?"

Lunedweth was standing over her.

"Yes."

The egg lurched again, and Lyf heard a soft ripping sound. There was a flurry of hail on the thatch, a tinkling of charms, a growling of distant thunder. The crack was longer now, and gaping. A tiny, translucent talon wiggled at one end of it, then vanished within the egg. Light spilled across it; Lyf looked up. Lunedweth was holding a candle.

Inside the egg Lyf could see something gray and glistening and wet. She could not tell if it was head or tail, if it was shoulder or stomach or leg.

The draclings crowded round now, thrumming, nosing at the egg. Lyf could feel their eagerness. Spens came and sat among them, stroking them, gazing at the egg.

"I don't know what to do," Lyf said.

Lunedweth shook her head. "Nor I. I know little of the Ancient Ones. But it doesn't take a dragon-sayer to know this: The hatchling will need a mother—and milk."

Milk! She spoke true. Kaeldra had said that the youngest

draclings needed milk. She said she had fed some of them goat's milk, but what they truly needed was the milk of a mother dragon.

Thunder boomed; the egg lurched again. Something was pushing up through the crack.

A nose.

Another lurch, and a tiny head poked out.

It was long and bony and all-over damp. It seemed to be covered with a clammy, fuzzy skin. Its eyes were squeezed tightly shut, and its little skinny pink forked tongue flicked in and out.

It was the *ugliest* thing Lyf had ever seen.

The head began to swivel round, nostrils flaring, as if the hatchling were trying to *feel* the world by smell. A sound. It was making a sound. A hoarse little squeaky sound, like a rusty hinge.

"Oh, sweet mother of the planets," Lunedweth said.

A clap of thunder. The loose shutter ripped off with a thump and the wind was blowing inside, riffling the pages of the books, stirring Lyf's hair. Lunedweth was shouting something at Spens, something about the shutter. Lyf saw Owyn stumbling sleepily toward her; he nestled in among the draclings, near the egg.

The hatchling struggled pitifully to free itself from its shell. Lyf was tempted to help it, to pry the egg away. But with chicks it was best to let them do it themselves. So too, perhaps, with draclings.

She watched.

The hatchling gave a great heave; the crack widened. Another heave, and the tiny body flopped through the gap, slid into Lyf's lap.

It was all skin and bones and talons—a piteous sight. Its

head seemed far too big for its body, far too heavy for its spindly neck to support. It lay on Lyf's lap, heaving for breath, its heartbeat pulsing in its throat.

The draclings surged closer, gazing at the hatchling. Lyf might have feared that they would harm it, were they not thrumming so loud.

She removed the shell from her lap then reached out a finger and stroked the hatchling, stroked all the way down its back and tail. She could feel the sharp little bones beneath the wet layer of fuzz. Her finger came away wet and creamy-feeling. It was like fleece-wax. Like touching a lamb's wool.

The hatchling twitched, flopped, staggered across Lyf's lap—nudging her, making little smacking, sucking sounds with its mouth.

"Here."

Lunedweth handed Lyf a twisted rag dripping with goat's milk. Lyf held it above the hatchling, let it drip onto the tiny snout. The hatchling snapped at the cloth and began to suckle. Lyf could see movement in its scrawny little throat as it swallowed. All around, the draclings leaned toward her, thrumming loud. The hatchling suckled but a short while, then sagged down again, asleep.

Now the thunder and wind had abated and settled down to a steady, hard rain. Spens, Lyf saw, was nailing the shutter back down.

She stroked the hatchling again. It had already begun to dry. Its skin felt soft—so soft. Its sides swelled with an intake of breath, then it gave a little sigh and melted deeper into Lyf's lap.

And a strong, warm feeling flooded Lyf: a fierceness, an urge to protect. This hatchling . . . she was bound to it in some way she did not understand. She was vulnerable now in a way she had never been. If harm befell this little one . . . well, she could not steel herself against it. She could not separate herself from it. It would pierce her to the bone.

"They hatch out of eggs, like birds," Lunedweth was musing, "but they take milk like humans, like goats. And yet I fear they're like birds in another way, as well."

"How is that?" Lyf asked.

"You're the first thing it saw, the first to feed it. This wee one thinks you're its mam."

Harper's Tale

When a rat scurries round you long enough, you begin to know the smell of it.

Their suspicions of Nysien grew. While Kaeldra rested and the others made ready to sail up the coast to the dragon's cave, Nysien scurried round the village in search of . . . what? Provisions, he said. Ever it was provisions.

And now, of a sudden, Nysien began to fret after Owyn and Lyf. He would ride out in search of them, he said. They might be lost, he said—or worse. "You sail on to the cave without me. Make a fire at the cave mouth. I'll find it."

The harper, thinking it well to keep Nysien under watch, made offer to go with him.

Both Nysien and Jeorg protested.

Later, Jeorg took the harper aside. He, Jeorg, would follow

Nysien, while Kaeldra and the harper and the fisherman went ahead. "I leave her in your care," he said.

He must truly have been alarmed to leave Kaeldra in the care of another—even one so illustrious as the harper.

But the trouble, my lords and ladies, was greater than he thought.

CHAPTER 16

Never You Fret

Lyf got little sleep for all the rest of that night. Every time she started to doze, the hatchling would let out its high, mewling *peep peep peep,* then nudge at her belly, making soft, sucking sounds. She kept a pig bladder full of goat's milk at her side. The other draclings did not clamor to drink it; they had sniffed it at first but seemed to have no taste for it. Lyf would squirt milk onto the cloth teat, then hold it over the hatchling's snout, letting the milk drip down. Once, Lunedweth tried to feed the hatchling too so that Lyf could get some sleep, but the hatchling hissed and stumbled blindly away from her, seeking out Lyf.

"It knows the smell of you," Lunedweth said, "and won't take food from any but its mam."

And now Lyf was truly caught. For so long she had yearned for the day when she could give the draclings to someone else—someone stronger, someone older, someone who could deliver them into the charge of a dragon full-grown. But this hatchling would not take food, save from her. She could not give it over to another—even Kaeldra—or the little one would starve. *She* would have to take it to the mother dragon.

And yet her fears were greatly blunted by the sweetness of having this little helpless creature in her lap, kneading and thrumming, taking nourishment from only her hands.

The draclings floated from time to time, rising up, jangling in the moons and stars, startling Lyf awake. Neither Luned-weth nor Spens remarked on it, though surely they heard. Likely they had seen the draclings float before, when Lyf had yet been tranced. Likely they were used to it by now.

It was nearly dawn when Lyf heard whispers.

"You must tell her!" she heard.

"But I *swore*. I gave my word."

"She's likely the one the secret's *for*. You must tell!"

Beyond the dim glow of the banked fire, Lyf could make out two shadowy forms crouched in a far corner.

"Tell what?" Lyf asked.

Silence. One of the forms moved: a rustle of cloth, the crunch of a foot in straw, a tinkling of silver. A tongue of light bloomed up from the embers, illuminated Lunedweth's face. "Come, Spens," she said, then came to kneel at the edge of the knobbly mound of draclings surrounding Lyf.

Spens crept slowly near, until the candlelight flickered across his face. A shock of dark hair fell across his brow. "I swore I wouldn't tell," he said.

"Don't be a muddlewit! He'll be vexed with you if you don't. And these . . ." Light bled across the draclings. They had sunk back to the ground, their sides moving peacefully in sleep breathing. "There's little enough chance for 'em. You must tell."

"Tell *what?*" Lyf asked. "*Who* will be vexed?"

No answer.

"Is it Kaeldra? Have you had word of her?"

"It's . . . my uncle," Spens said at last. "He's a fisherman in the village of Merdoc. There's a . . . a dove carved on his boat."

The breath caught in Lyf's throat. "A dove?"

"One time I was pointing out his boat to someone, and I said, ' 'Tis the one with the dove on its prow.' And my uncle nearly barked me down. After, I mean. I was not to speak of it, he said. And I said, 'Anyone could see it. It's plain to view.' And he said they wouldn't remark upon it, 'less it were pointed out. And then when you spoke of the brine rats, well, I saw some in his boat once, in a fish barrel. And I asked about them, and he said the same thing. Made me swear not to breathe a word. And he wouldn't tell me why."

Relief flooded through her. One of the dove sign!

"Is it near, this Merdoc?" Lyf asked. "Can we go there?"

"Not now," Lunedweth said. "Sleep while yet you can! There are things I must attend to—then we'll see."

Soon enough, Lyf woke to the hatchling's hungry mewlings. Sleepily, she fed it. She could not tell whether this hatchling was male or female. In the faint morning light, its skin looked gray—neither reddish gray nor greenish gray—and it was whole, without rents to show the scales beneath. Lyf tried to ken with it, but felt only a faint tingling in her head. The hatchling's scrawny throat worked as it swallowed, its face suffused with bliss. Watching, Lyf was engulfed by a wave of tenderness.

She could see Owyn asleep among the draclings, and Spens's slumbering form on his pallet. Lunedweth was tending a small fire in a clay bowl by the window. Smoke twined up in odd undulations, and the fresh, pungent smell of burning tinewort filled the room. Lunedweth began to chant—softly, rhythmically, waving her purple-tipped fingers above the flame, disturbing the smoke. At last she stopped, doused the flame with water, and turned to face Lyf.

"You must go now," she said, "for the earth pulse conspires against you in this place. I sense a warping in the aura, and the moon is out of phase. Besides," she added, "something's come into the marsh. The birds are in a pother—and I'm certain I heard dogs."

They made their way through the marsh while mist shrank the world to a moving patch of gray water and ghostly reeds. Though Lyf was fearful, straining eyes and ears against the mist for signs of men and dogs, the going was easier than before. For Spens conveyed them in his boat—a stout, leathern tub of a vessel, hardly large enough to contain them all. He knelt astern and rowed while Lyf and Owyn sat forward amid a welter of squirming draclings. The hatchling slumbered within the carrier; when she pressed it to her stomach, Lyf could feel it thrum.

She marked no sign of others in the marsh—though it was true that she could see little beyond the gray pall of fog. She did hear birds, but there were ever birds in the marsh. Twice she thought she heard barking.

"Never you fret," Spens said, reassuring. "I know these marshlands as well as my own left knee. If the hunters come near, I know channels they'll never find, and bolt-holes they'd never dream of."

Lunedweth did not come. She stood watching and faded

behind them into the mist until she and her crannog and her hut had vanished away entire.

"Will they find her?" Lyf asked Spens. "Whoever it is with the dogs?"

"Not soon," he said. "But when the fog burns off . . ."

Spens had argued with Lunedweth to put out her fire so that the smoke would not betray her whereabouts. But she had refused. "I'll draw them away from you," she had said. "I'll mix them a love potion in a cup of plum wine—no—I'll not have them clinging to me. I'll cast a muddlement on them. They'll stagger round the marsh till you're well away."

Yet whoever it was would likely find Lunedweth, soon or late. And though Lunedweth had sworn she would cast a muddlement on them, Lyf gravely doubted whether she could cast anything but sticks and stones. Lyf wondered again that Lunedweth would help them, would risk her life for theirs. "*You were needin' help, so I gave it. It's that simple. If you can't understand that, then I pity you—so I do.*"

At first the draclings were restless. Clambering one on top of another, they swarmed in a wiggly heap to one side of the boat and then the other. They peered down into the rippling water, huffed out smoke at the rushes passing by. Lyf scolded them to be still, because the boat was tipping precariously. Smoak sprang into her lap and hiccuped smoky breaths into her face. Only the hatchling slept.

Owyn wanted to peek at it; Lyf opened the sack and let him look in. "Be gentle with it, now," she said.

With a great show of tenderness, he reached his chubby hand within the sack and stroked the hatchling's head. "It's soft," he said. Satisfied, he withdrew his hand; he paid little mind to the hatchling after that.

But Lyf could not get enough of it. Again and again she opened the sack and peered within. Movement flickered beneath the hatchling's eyelids, and expressions poured like water over its bony face: joy, and then pain, and then joy again. Dreaming, it was. But what, Lyf wondered, did one so new to this world have to dream of?

The hatchling sneezed, breathed in sharply, let out a long, slow sigh.

So helpless.

So sweet.

Kindle jealously butted at Lyf whenever she gazed down at the hatchling, until Lyf relented and scratched between Kindle's eye ridges. Then the little blue-green dracling closed her eyes, thrumming, and the corners of her mouth curved up in a smile.

Lunedweth had mixed in a sleeping potion with the draclings' meal of dried newts, and soon, much to Lyf's relief, it took effect. Before long the draclings settled down into a tangled, drowsy heap in the bottom of the boat. Spens tossed Lyf a fishnet; she spread it over them.

But Owyn was not tired a bit. He kept plaguing her with questions and complaints—"Why do we have to go *now?*" "Why can't Lunie come with us?" "When will we get to the town?" "I'm hungry!" "I'm thirsty!" "My legs hurt!"

Lyf answered his questions, urged him to have patience, rubbed his cramping legs. But soon she felt herself begin to fade. She had not been quite the same since that last kenning. She felt drained all the time and seemed to need more sleep. Her thoughts often came muzzy and dull.

At last, in spite of Owyn, in spite of her trepidations, Lyf drowsed off. When she opened her eyes, the mist had dispersed. The boat was scudding down a brisk stream surrounded by forest. The draclings still slept; Owyn had somehow moved back near Spens, who deftly guided the boat through the churning water. Spens smiled, seeing Lyf awake, as he answered one of Owyn's *whys*.

The hatchling was mewling. Lyf sat up, groped about for the bladder of goat's milk Lunedweth had given her, and began to feed it.

"Have you seen anyone?" she asked. "The men with the dogs?"

"Nary a soul," Spens said.

"Why are you sleeping so much?" Owyn asked.

"I was . . . sick," Lyf said. "But I'm feeling better now."

And she *did* feel better—less drained, less muzzy. But she was still tired. When the hatchling had done with feeding, she snuggled against the netted heap of draclings and closed her eyes again.

When next she awoke, it was nearly dusk. "Have I slept so long?" she murmured, looking about her. The river had widened now. Calmed. It was lined on both banks with scrubby tanlar trees, but beyond them she saw planted fields.

Spens chuckled. "You've slept nearly all this day."

"I *never* sleep so long," she said. The kenning. It must have been that. The draclings, awake and restless, came thrumming toward her. Someone had taken off their net. Owyn started drumming on the boat with a spoon Lunedweth had given him.

"Have they been fed?" Lyf asked.

Spens nodded. "Dried lizards for the draclings—the last of Lunedweth's cache. Some of her stewed meat"—he wrinkled his nose—"for Owyn and me. Would you be wantin' some?"

Lyf shook her head. She wasn't ready for Lunedweth's cooking. Not yet. Her stomach felt too unsettled. But her mind, for the first time since the kenning, was clear.

Spens, she saw now, had turned the boat and was paddling in toward shore.

"We'll wait in a place I know," he said, "till after dark. The village isn't far. I hope my uncle's home. My aunt . . . well . . . I've never spoken to her of . . . the dove sign."

Lyf felt a flicker of unease.

"But she *must* know," Spens said. "And besides, my uncle's likely home. Never you fret."

Spens grabbed an overhanging root when they reached shore; the draclings surged out of the boat and scrambled onto the bank. Lyf gave Owyn a boost, then picked up the bladder of milk and clambered up herself. The river held a dull, pewter gleam, but darkness lay thick among the trees. Spens dragged the boat up the slope and stowed it in a heap of brush. He led them along the shaded riverbank, then up a long, sloping path until they came to a stone-built hut set into the side of the hill.

"It's years since I've been here," he said. "My friends and I, we used to bide here sometimes. It was our fort."

The sharp smell of moldering thatch engulfed Lyf as she entered. The shed had no windows, but light seeped in through a gap in one wall and a yawning hole in the roof. Owyn threw himself down on the packed-earth floor; the draclings bounded in after, walked across his stomach, flicked at him with forked tongues.

The hatchling was peeping for milk, but when Lyf began to feed it, Kindle climbed into her lap and nipped at the milk rag.

<No!> Lyf said. She dumped Kindle off her lap and yanked at the rag.

Kindle bit down on the rag, then backed away, ripping it.

"No!" Lyf jerked hard on the rag.

Kindle reared up, spat out a spray of sparks at the hatchling, who broke into frenzied peeping.

Lyf lunged for Kindle, but the dracling streaked away to a far corner of the hut. She looked back reproachfully, then lay down with her chin on her talons.

If Kindle had her way, Lyf thought, *the hatchling would starve.*

Lyf fed the hatchling the last of the milk, keeping her glance carefully averted from Kindle, trying to ignore the odd little aching in her chest.

They waited. Owyn began to drum on the walls with his spoon. The draclings, restless, romped about the shed, bumping into Lyf and Owyn and Spens in playful skirmishing. Skorch always came out on top in a fray; he could cow most of the others by simply spitting sparks.

Soon, the draclings were flying. The elder ones were better skilled. They could spiral up into the air, flit neatly through the hole in the thatch and, huffing out a steady flame, float down to alight on their feet. Lyf fretted that they might be seen above the hut, but Spens assured her that no one ever came near this place. "And the trees are too tall and too thick for the flame light to be seen," he said.

The middle-sized draclings were clumsier, with many jerky ups and downs, many chin-and-belly landings, many perilous gouts of flame. It was good that the hut was stone-built, or they would surely have set it afire.

Kindle's wings had come all the way unfurled: thin and gossamer as damselfly wings. She floated timidly, close to the ground, tentatively fluttering one wing and then the other.

Dusk shaded slowly into night. A gibbous moon bleached the sky to luminous gray. Below, in the hut, all was dark.

"Let's be going," Spens said.

Taking Owyn by the hand, Lyf followed Spens back down the path, then along the tree-lined riverbank. The draclings bounded along behind. But Kindle made no move to climb up on Lyf's shoulders. And, though Lyf had often wished for the sake of her aching neck that Kindle would get down and walk, she found now that she missed her.

It's just as well, Lyf told herself. *Kindle might do harm to the hatchling.*

Through the pungent fragrance of the tanlars, Lyf caught a faint whiff of fish and salt and tar. They were very near the sea. Before long, Spens halted. Peering through the trees ahead, Lyf spied a stone bridge spanning the river.

"We'll cross—" Spens began, then, "Wait!"

Lyf heard it then—a rumbling of hooves. They were nearing, coming this way.

"Get down!" Spens said.

Lyf crouched low, holding Owyn beside her. <Still!> she told the draclings. <Be still!>

They crowded in close about her, thrumming, sniffing at the air.

The rumbling rose to a loud, hollow drumming. She could see them now, coming out of the trees ahead and pounding across the bridge: horses dark, capes billowing behind, torches streaming trails of yellow light.

Soldiers.

A whinny. A rearing horse. It lit down, shied away. There was a curse, a voice she knew. In the light of a passing torch, Lyf saw him: thin, dark-haired, beak-nosed, and capeless.

Nysien. He was with them. He was riding with the Krags.

Harper's Tale

Unbeknownst to Kaeldra and her friends, the queen's men had followed them ever since they had left the castle. Nysien had shown the way. For he knew that Kaeldra would never lead the soldiers to dragons—unless she did so without knowing.

Unbeknownst to Jeorg, he was stalked whilst stalking Nysien. The soldiers knocked him on the head. They stowed him bound, gagged, and senseless in a heap of brush.

Unbeknownst to Kaeldra, the queen had had new tone pipes forged for the trancing of the dragons. Her men were schooled in the use of them by a soldier from years before.

Much, my lords, was unbeknownst.

And what of Lyf, you ask? You say I *never* tell of Lyf?

It was unbeknownst, my lady!

(But save me a bit of that roast, and perhaps it will be known to you soon.)

Chapter 17

Borrowed Troubles

"This way!" Spens said when the soldiers had disappeared over a rise to the north.

Lyf stood gaping after, the sound of hoofbeats still drumming in her ears.

Nysien. With the soldiers. What could that bode?

Might *Kaeldra* have been with them?

"Lyf, come *along!*" Spens plucked at her sleeve, urged her up over an embankment, onto the road. She reached for Owyn's hand and summoned the draclings.

"Spens! I saw—"

"Sh!" Spens led them over the bridge. Now Lyf could see the town to the south—dark houses against darker earth—and directly west before them the gleaming, veined delta where the river met the sea. She hurried, for there was no hiding on the bridge; the line of romping draclings would be clear to view.

They followed Spens as he scrambled off the road on the other side, backtracked along the river through the trees, then waded through a field of rye behind the town. At last he turned into a back lane, veered off into an alley, crossed a cobbled street. "Come on, now!" he said. "We're home!"

He pushed on the door; it didn't budge. He assailed it with a flurry of raps.

"Sh!" Lyf said. She glanced anxiously at the nearby cottages, then up at the lintel.

No dove.

The door creaked open. A woman peered out. By the dim light that seeped through the doorway, Lyf could see that her eyes were small and anxious, her lips pursed tight.

"Spens!" she hissed. "Get you within, and be quick about it! Cletus has gone; now's no time to be abroad. Make haste now, get—" She stopped, looked past Spens to Lyf, then Owyn. Lyf knew the moment her gaze reached the draclings, for her scalp lifted and she moved her hand in the sign against evil.

"Get them away from here!" she whispered hoarsely. "We can't be caught with them! The soldiers—"

"But Auntie, Uncle Cletus wouldn't turn them out. I know about the dove sign now. I know what he's been doing."

"Shoo! Shoo! Away with you!" Spens's aunt pushed past him, brandishing a broom at the draclings.

Spens grabbed the broom. "Auntie, stop! We'll be discovered. You've got to take them in, or Uncle Cletus will be wroth!"

"If Cletus chooses to risk his own neck, there's no stopping him. But I *won't* do so, and neither will you. Don't be borrowing their troubles and making them yours. Now, shoo!" She wrenched the broom out of Spens's hands and advanced upon the draclings. They backed away, huffing out smoke—all but Skorch, who stood his ground.

"He'll burn it!" Lyf warned. "He *hates* brooms!"

Spens's aunt rounded on Lyf and Owyn, shook the broom at them. "And you two as well! Git! We can't be havin' you here!"

"Auntie!" Spens was aghast.

"They're searchin' for them, Spens!" she said. "Them and their beasties. They're a peril to us all!"

Skorch lunged at Spens's aunt, breathed out a lick of flame.

"No, Skorch!" Lyf lunged forward, threw her arms about Skorch's neck, tried to drag him away. He strained against her, snorting out smoke.

Spens's aunt opened her mouth to scream, but no sound came out. Blue flame crept along the edge of her sleeve. She roused, flung down the broom, and beat at the flame with her skirt. Then she bolted within the cottage and slammed the door behind.

Lyf stared at the door, her arms still about Skorch. Her mind was numb. Slow.

Spens was saying something, was stumbling through the press of draclings into the alley. Lyf heard doors opening, heard voices. A torch flared in the shadows down the street. She leapt to her feet, snatched Owyn's hand, and ran after Spens; the draclings swarmed behind.

"I've friends in this town," Spens said when they caught up to him in the alley. "Never you fret."

"I think they saw us!" Lyf said. "Those folk in the street." Little use his friends would be if the whole town raised hue and cry.

"You go back to the hut. I'll come after, with help."

Lyf ran through the dark alley into the lane, still clutching Owyn's hand. The draclings flocked after them. She heard voices back where they had been. She came out into the field and made a dash for the river, hugging the hatchling with one arm so that it would not thump against her belly, pulling Owyn through the waist-deep rye. It was not until they reached the tanlar trees that she dared to look back.

In the moonlight, the field looked smooth, undisturbed by movement. None, so far as she could tell, had pursued them. Maybe they *hadn't* seen. Or maybe Spens had managed to forestall them. The draclings crowded about her, rubbing against her legs. She could feel their agitation, as surely they felt hers.

<Hush,> she told them soothingly. <All's well.>

"I want my mama," Owyn said. "I want to go home."

"Oh, Owyn." Lyf knelt to hug him. "So do I. But we can't, just yet."

"Why?"

Lyf took thought, tried truly to *answer* him this time. "Because the draclings will be killed if we go home right now. We have to find a mama for them. Then we can find *your* mama." She held him at arm's length, studied his face. "Do you understand?"

Owyn nodded gravely. And he did understand—she could see it. She was struck anew with the certainty that there was more going on beneath that grubby little brow than she credited him with. She hugged him again, feeling the solid bulk of him, blinking back the tears that, unbidden, sprang into her eyes. He had been a stout companion to her, all this long while.

They edged along the river through the tanlars until they

were nearly at the bridge. Lyf hesitated. They would have to leave the sheltering trees to cross it.

Wait.

Voices. Deep voices.

They came not from town or road or fields, but from upriver.

Soldiers? But she had seen the soldiers leaving town.

Lyf crouched behind a mass of thorny bushes, pulled Owyn down beside her. "Hush!" she said to Owyn and, to the draclings, <Lie down!> Skorch stretched out on the ground beside her; the others did likewise.

Now, through the web of branches, Lyf could see something on the river: a boat. Another. Yet another. Voices. Elythian voices. The boats drew near, passed straight before them. Moonlight glinted on a crossbow, the hilt of a sheathed sword, a quiver of arrows.

Bounty hunters.

Lyf waited until they disappeared beyond the bridge, until she could no longer hear their voices. Then she waited more—but not *too* long. That door she had heard opening, those voices in the village . . . They might come searching soon.

Lyf took Owyn's hand and fled across the bridge, expecting to be cried out at any moment. She plunged into the darkness among the tanlars beyond. Her heart pounded in her throat. The draclings thronged about her legs.

Silence.

Only the sounds of the river.

More slowly now they made their way back to the hut and huddled together in the dim light within, waiting.

Owyn curled up and slept, his head on her lap. The draclings slumbered too, thrumming softly. But Lyf was strung too taut for sleep. Her ears strained into the silence of the night. Every snap of a twig, every rustling of leaves set her heart pounding with hope and terror. Hope that it was Spens. Terror that it might be another.

The hatchling began to peep. Lyf scrabbled round to find the bladder and tried to squeeze more milk from it, but only a few drops splashed down on the hatchling's snout. The peeping grew weaker, subsided. Lyf stroked the little one's head, reached down into the carrier to cup its fuzzy belly. Its breath rose weakly—too weakly.

It needed milk.

At last she heard footfalls purposefully nearing. The door creaked open.

It was Spens.

Lyf let out a grateful breath.

In the thin moonlight that sifted down through the broken roof, Lyf could see that his eyes looked bruised, as if he had been crying. He waded through the mass of draclings and came to sit silently by her. "They wouldn't help," he said at last. "They turned me away, each last one of them."

Lyf was frightened. What would they do now? And another thing: those bounty hunters. "Your friends . . . wouldn't tell, would they? That we're here?"

"No, they never would! Or . . . I don't think so. Anyway, I didn't tell them where we're hiding. But I never thought they'd send us away." Spens turned to her . "I'm sorry, Lyf. I *thought* I had friends."

"You do have friends; it's just . . . just *us*." Lyf gestured at the draclings. "We're beyond what they can bear."

"If they were truly friends, they would have helped."

Lyf did not know what to say. He seemed so wretched.

She touched his shoulder, briefly. "The wonder," she said, "is not that folk would turn us away, but that there are folk like you to borrow our troubles and make them yours." And like Yanil and Kymo and Lunedweth, she added to herself. And Alys. Alys, who had thought that she *owed*. "You're risking your life for us," Lyf said. "I could never do that. I'd run away." She *had* run away, Lyf remembered.

"But you're doin' it already—for *them*." He motioned toward the draclings.

"That's different. I've no choice in it. They won't let me get away."

"You could give them to the hunters."

"No!"

"You *could*, though. But you don't. You've taken their troubles on yourself."

Lyf thought about that. It was true, she supposed. She didn't choose to take on their troubles, but now that she had, she wouldn't abandon them. Couldn't. She could not even imagine doing so.

She peered down at the hatchling in its sack. It breathed in a shaky breath, whistling softly. With a finger, Lyf stroked its bony head. She thought back to the start of her journey, when she had refused to fetch water for Kymo. What a sniveler he must have thought her!

Spens broke into her musings. "I went back to my aunt," he said. "She told me Kaeldra came last night with her husband and a harper and—"

"Kaeldra—here? And *free*?"

Spens nodded.

Lyf breathed in deep, seemed to fill up with hope. "Where is she? Why didn't you bring her here?"

"She's gone with my uncle up the coast to the cave. They thought you and the draclings might be there. Her husband came here with them, and a harper, and some kinsman or other—"

"Kinsman? What kinsman?"

"I don't know. Somebody's husband, I think."

"Our sister's husband? Nysien?"

"Yes, that's the one. And they . . ."

Nysien. Lyf had forgotten about Nysien. Spens was still talking, but she couldn't attend. All the hope within her was shrinking, shrinking to a hard, cold knot.

"So, Nysien rode up to the cave with Kaeldra?" she asked.

"No! I just told you—Kaeldra and my uncle and the harper went there in my uncle's boat. Nysien and Kaeldra's husband stayed behind, but my aunt doesn't know where. And then the soldiers came riding into the village, and my aunt was afeared. She said . . ." Spens hesitated. "She said some of them were boasting, sticking their hands with knives. She said they didn't bleed."

Lyf recoiled. *Invulnerable to sharp metal.* Was it true then? The little draclings . . .

But no. It wouldn't *have* to have been the little draclings. It could have been some other dragon. Their mother. But . . . the little ones had died—Lyf owned it to herself now. She knew this from the pain she had felt.

Tears welled in her eyes. But there was something she must tell Spens.

"I saw Nysien with soldiers, on the road going out of town."

"You saw him? Why didn't you say?"

"I tried, but you never listened."

"What would he be doing with the soldiers? Leading them away?"

"No," Lyf said. "He betrayed Kaeldra. But I don't think she knows."

"*Betrayed?* Why?"

"For gold," Lyf said simply.

Spens opened his mouth as if to ask another question, then shut it, took thought, spoke again. "That road they took goes north. It curves along the coast. I doubt the soldiers could see the cave from the road, but they could find it by my uncle's boat. It would be anchored nearby."

"So she'll lead them straight to the dragon."

Spens nodded grimly. "And if we try to warn her, and take the draclings with us, we'll be walking into the trap. But we can't be stayin' here. Did you see those hunters? They came into the village after you left. They were searching for us."

"I saw them."

"I hope that Lunedweth—" Spens broke off.

Lyf hoped as well. For Lunedweth. For Alys. But for the two little draclings, she could only mourn.

Footsteps, outside the door.

"Spens?"

The door creaked ajar. The draclings' heads snapped up, alert, their gazes fixed on the doorway. In the shadows, Lyf saw a girl's face—heart shaped, with wide-set, intelligent eyes.

Spens leapt to his feet. "Aura!"

"Will they harm me?" she asked. "The draclings?"

Spens turned to Lyf. "This is Aura. My *friend*. They won't harm her, now, will they?"

They had not hurt to Spens, nor any other they had met—

until Spens's aunt. The memory of that still burned in Lyf's mind.

"I don't think they'll do you harm," Lyf said. "But move slowly. Stay by the door till they grow used to you."

Aura did not look reassured. "I *thought* you'd be here," she said to Spens.

"But your da said you'd none of you help."

"I disobeyed him. I—and Donal and the twins."

Two more faces appeared in the doorway—a boy and a girl of seven winters or so. Aura was older. Her own age, Lyf guessed.

"Donal's gone to fetch Turi." Aura held up a sack. "Here. Likely you'll need food."

It was the food that placated the draclings—especially the cheese. They loved cheese. At first they were leery of the children. They arched their backs, snorting out smoke. But when Aura set a chunk of cheese on the ground, Skorch ventured slowly forward and sniffed at it. He took it up in his talons, turned it over, flicked at it with his forked tongue. Then he gulped it down whole. The other draclings swarmed about Aura, butting their heads against her legs, thrumming, begging for more.

Yet, still, the draclings were warier of strangers now than they had been. And, after what had passed with Spens's aunt, Lyf could not be at ease. Their fire . . . it was perilous. How if a child by mischance stepped on a dracling's tail?

And another worry—one she could not tell Spens. He seemed so sure of these friends of his—but *could* they be trusted? And what if someone had followed without their knowing?

Owyn roused at the smell of food, and Aura fed him, too,

exclaiming over this thatch of red-gold hair, his freckles, his snub of a nose. He snuggled sleepily beside her, content, for once, to be fussed over.

The twins, it seemed, were Aura's younger siblings. Their older brother, Donal, had gone to find a friend. In spring and summer, the children often slept in the barn behind their cottage, so they had easily slipped away. "Though how Turi will do it, I don't know," Aura said. "And there's a stir in the village. Folk are seeking you out."

Lyf tried to feed the hatchling some of the cheese but, though it roused and sniffed, it would not eat. It peeped feebly once or twice, then sank back into sleep. It needed a mother—a dragon mother with milk—or it wouldn't live long. Nor would the others. They couldn't hide forever. Soon enough they would be found and slain.

Now the door creaked open again, and two boys edged warily within. "How did you slip away?" Aura demanded.

One of the boys shrugged and grinned. "It's not the first time."

"No one saw you?" Lyf asked quickly.

The boy turned his crooked grin upon her. "And nice it is to meet you, too. I'm Donal. And I know how to get about without being followed."

The draclings converged, thrumming, upon the newcomers—hoping, Lyf guessed, for more cheese. Uncertainly, the boys backed away. "Do you have food?" Lyf asked.

Donal held up a burlap sack. "Only a bag of whisple nuts."

"Give some to the draclings!"

He reached into the sack and flung out handfuls of nuts; there was a wild scramble as draclings chased the small round nuts all over the shed. Lyf watched, uneasy. *It will be well,* she told herself. *They won't do harm to Spens's friends. And Spens's friends won't do harm to us. He trusts them, and so must I.*

As the tumult subsided, Spens told the others what he and Lyf had surmised about the soldiers.

"But couldn't the mother dragon just *burn* them?" Donal asked. "I hear a dragon full-grown can burn a score of men!"

"True—unless the soldiers have tone pipes," Lyf said.

"Tone pipes?"

"Silver pipes. They make a sound that . . . trances the dragons. The soldiers breathe at different times, so the sound goes on without a break."

"They had them!" Turi said. "I saw one! A soldier was polishing it while he watered his horse. A little silver pipe."

Lyf swallowed hard. They had to stop them! But she didn't know how. Nor, judging from the silence, did the others.

Owyn, now fully awake, began marching round the edge of the shed, drumming with his spoon on a rusty old cowbell he had dredged up from somewhere. It was loud and harsh and irksome.

"Cease with that, Owyn," Lyf said. "You'll give us away. Besides, I can't hear my own thoughts."

Aura turned to her. "What did you say?"

"I told Owyn to cease with his drumming."

"No—after that."

"I said I can't hear my own thoughts."

"How if," Aura said slowly, "we made a clamorous noise? So the dragon couldn't *hear* the pipes? Then she'd be free to fight."

"But how would we get to the cave?" Donal wanted to know. "The soldiers have the lead of us by far."

"Turi, you have a boat," Spens said. "Is it big enough for all of us?"

"Not likely." Turi shrugged. "Besides, it's the slowest tub in the sea."

"We could borrow one," Aura said.

"Borrow?"

"They *hang* people for that!"

"They wouldn't hang *us*—we're but children!"

Turi snorted. "Even so, my da would beat me to within an inch of my life."

"Our ma'd keep us tethered within the house until well past childbearing!" said Aura's sister, Brynn. "I'd *rather* have a beating!"

"Aye, but if we stopped the Krags," Aura broke in, "they'd likely give us a medal!"

A burst of derisive laughter. "Medal, ha!"

"Aye, but if we *did* . . ."

Lyf didn't know when *if* gave way to *will*, but soon all were scouring the shed for more noise-making implements. They found only three horseshoes, a rusted-through weeding hook, and an old, broken hoop from a cask.

"No mind," Spens said. "There'll be pots and cups and spoons and such in the boat."

They ventured across the bridge and skirted the fields, staying as far from the village as they might. The sun had not risen, but a wash of faint light seeped up from the horizon into the eastern sky. Yet, in the end there was no avoiding the village. They must go through it to come to the harbor.

Spens led them through the dark lanes and alleys. The children came behind. Aura held Owyn's hand, whispering often into his ear. Lyf came last, with her escort of draclings.

From time to time they heard voices, and once they caught sight of men passing on a street up ahead. Spens motioned them into the gap between two cottages. Lyf, not daring to breathe, urged the draclings to be still. When the men had gone from view, Spens veered into another alley and guided them away.

The fish-and-salt smell of the sea grew strong. Spens turned round a corner, and then the harbor opened up before them. A pier jutted out into the bay; fishing boats clung to it like suckling pigs. They rocked, creaking in the early-morning swells. They looked deserted.

Spens led the children, nearly every one on tiptoe, down the pier. The draclings thronged about Lyf's feet, all but tripping her as she followed. And now she could see Spens near a boat at the end of the pier, helping the children in. She was two boats away when she heard a loud *thunk*, then a cry. Draclings surged past her, jostling the children, trampling Brynn, who had stumbled and sprawled out on the pier. A new sound; Lyf whirled round to find the source of it. And a sleepy, grizzle-bearded man stood up in the boat nearest her, rubbing his eyes.

He gaped, rubbed his eyes again, hissed out a curse. Then, "Dragons!" he shouted. "I've found them! The wolf's head's mine—so it is!"

Harper's Tale

There were three of them set sail in a fishing boat, bound north up the coast for the dragon's cave: Kaeldra, a fisherman named Cletus, and the finest harper this world has ever known.

Kaeldra, my lords and ladies, was full of aches. Her belly ached from the child within, from the tossing of the sea, from the sickness she had had. Her heart ached for Jeorg; she wished he had not stayed behind. She ached to know whether the dragons remained within the cave, or whether it was too late. And most of all, she ached with a fierce, burning hope to find Lyf and Owyn in the cave.

This hope, of course, was dashed. Lyf was not in the cave.

Where was she, you ask?

Patience, my lady, is a virt—Wait! Don't throw that! I *swear* I am coming to Lyf next.

Chapter 18

Swimming on the Wind

Lyf stumbled forward, careening into the throng of children and draclings. She helped the fallen Brynn to her feet, delivered her into a pair of hands within the boat, and then clambered within herself. Draclings were hurtling into the boat all around her. The gap between boat and pier widened. They had cast off. She heard Spens calling out orders and, looking round, found him astern at the tiller.

The grizzle-bearded man was still shouting; neither draclings nor children remained on the pier. Good. Lyf heard a hissing of ropes and, glancing up, saw that the sails had been raised.

"We're luffing!" Spens yelled. "Sheet in!"

The boat lurched. Lyf pitched to one side and fell into a heap of children and draclings. She scanned the crowd until her glance fell on a thatch of reddish hair. Owyn was nestled contentedly in Aura's arms. A little stab of jealousy pierced Lyf. For so long she had looked for someone to take care of him, but now that someone was . . .

Draclings came crowding around her, thrumming. Kindle climbed up and settled about her neck. Lyf scratched her eye ridges. Kindle lifted her chin, and Lyf scratched in the hollow beneath her jaw. The dracling thrummed and kneaded Lyf's shoulders with her talons. It was good to have her back.

The hatchling poked its head out of its sack and peeped at Kindle. Kindle hissed at it.

"Stop it, Kindle," Lyf said. "No!"

The hatchling peeped again. Kindle arched her back, spat out a lick of flame.

"No!" Lyf grabbed Kindle, tossed her into the heap of draclings. Kindle snorted out smoke, then burrowed beneath the heap until only her twitching tail could be seen.

Lyf sighed, then checked the hatchling for burns; it seemed unharmed. She stood and searched the bay behind them. The deck rolled beneath her feet. Wind whipped strands of loose hair about her face.

No sails.

But back on the pier, a crowd had gathered. As Lyf watched, another boat pulled away.

Clinging to the gunwale, she made her way back to where Spens stood astern. "Can we outrun them?" she asked.

Spens shrugged. "We've got a good start of them."

"But didn't you . . . borrow . . . the fastest boat?"

"She's reputed so. But I don't know her—know all the ins and outs of sailing her. They"—he jerked his head toward the pier—"will know *their* boats full well."

"Boats?" Lyf was puzzled. "There's but one."

"There will be more," Spens said grimly. "We've stolen this one, haven't we? Even folk who wouldn't turn us over to the Krags will come for us now. And that man did see the draclings. The wolf's head—any man who captures them will make himself the richest in Merdoc."

Before long they were out of the bay and sailing up the coast. The wind picked up, tangled in Lyf's hair, flung salt spray into her eyes. Out here the seas were rough and capped with white. Lyf clung to the gunwale as the little boat tipped and pitched. The draclings had gathered together amidships in a woozy heap that slithered to one side of the boat and then the other. Some were fast asleep, but others, jarred awake, spat out angry licks of flame. Lyf prayed that nothing would catch fire. She feared as well that the draclings might try to fly but, perhaps because of the wind, none did.

The children, save for those handling tiller and sail, sat together near the draclings. One of the twins had raided the galley and handed out pots and pans and a jumble of iron cooking tools. Aura motioned to Lyf, then scooted aside to make room for her. The children waved and called, "Ho, Lyf!" as she stumbled across the heaving deck. When she had wedged herself into the small space next to Aura and Owyn, someone handed her a hunk of bread. She started to offer some to Owyn, but his mouth was already full, so she ate the bread herself.

"May I see the hatchling?" Aura asked. Lyf leaned toward her; Aura peered into the carrier. "Will it flame at me if I touch it?" she asked.

Lyf shook her head. "It doesn't flame yet, I'm thinking."

Tentatively, Aura drew a finger along the hatchling's snout. She pulled her hand away, then smiled at Lyf. "It's fuzzy."

Lyf nodded.

Someone started up a song about a daring venture, and they all joined in. Aura offered her a wineskin; Lyf took a sip and passed it along. Spray flew in great white sheets over the gunwales; Lyf was drenched from crown to toe. And yet, she felt . . . *warm,* somehow, crowded in among these strangers who had become companions. Who had become *friends*.

Lyf thought of the other friends she had made along the way. Kymo. Yanil. Lunedweth. Alys. They had had no good reason for helping her and Owyn and the draclings—and yet they *had* done so. To their peril. Perhaps to their harm. Lyf drew in a deep, salty breath and felt . . . *gratitude* welling up inside her. Whatever happened now, she would not forget them. Not ever.

The hatchling was making sad little whining squeaks. Lyf tried to get it to eat a piece of bread, but it sniffed and turned away. If only she had more goat's milk! "You should have taken that cheese," she scolded. "You shouldn't be so choosy." Worry tugged at her. How often did it need to eat? And how if the mother dragon had already flown—or been killed? The hatchling seemed frightfully weak now. Its skin looked dull and shriveled; it could barely lift its head.

She felt the heat of another gaze upon her and turned to see Kindle staring at her from the welter of draclings. <You can come here, Kindle,> Lyf told her, <but only if you're good. If you don't do harm to the little one.> Kindle made no move to come, but only looked at her with mournful eyes.

When Lyf turned back now, she could see other sails.

Four of them. Seven. Twelve sails coming behind. The coastline grew more and more rugged; in time the land rose in sheer, rocky cliffs. Spens guided the boat in closer to shore, and Lyf could see that the cliffs were pocked with crannies and caves.

How would they know the right one?

"Look there!"

Some of the children were pointing. When Lyf followed the direction of their hands, she marked something in the sky above the land, a dark smudge on the horizon.

Smoke. It must be smoke. What would make smoke up here? Dragons? Soldiers? Kaeldra?

"Hurry!" Lyf said under her breath.

But there was no hurrying the wind. The boat, tacking this way and then that, seemed to *crawl* toward the source of the smoke.

Still, next time Lyf looked back, she saw with alarm that some of the boats *did* seem to be hurrying. One was approaching so near that she could make out the shapes of its crew.

Hurry!

They rounded a bluff. The wind freshened, tore at Lyf's hair and clothes, spewed spray into her eyes. The seas loomed high, capped with froth. Lyf searched for the smoke but could no longer find it; the cliff blotted everything out.

A shout from behind. Lyf whirled round. The other boat was bearing down fast. She could see the men's features now: eyes and yelling mouths. She stared numbly as the boat drew nearer, nearer. It was pulling alongside.

A scraping sound. Hands were grabbing the gunwale; children were shrieking. A big, burly man flung a leg over.

He was in.

Then at once Skorch was there before him, belching out fire. The man swore, threw himself backward into his boat. His shirt was ablaze. Someone doused him with a bucket of water, but now Skorch flamed again—harder. The men screamed and ducked as a gout of blue fire shot over their heads and engulfed their sail. A flurry of shouting and jostling; they were flinging water up at the sail. Lyf's boat sped. All around her, children cheered.

But Lyf did not cheer. She stood gaping at Skorch, terrified and awed. He had nearly *killed* that man.

And then they were rounding another bluff. Aura tugged on Lyf's elbow, pointing up. "Look!"

Something ahead, atop the next bluff. Men. In red capes. The soldiers—a whole long row of them, lining the edge of the cliff. Some were dangling from ropes—climbing down.

And there it was, where the cliff met the water—the mouth of an enormous cave. Smoke trailed out of it, twisted into the sky.

Kaeldra—she must be there. All at once Lyf ached to see her—*now*. It had been so long. She had feared she would never see her again.

A glinting caught Lyf's eye. A piercing, silvery sound . . .

Tone pipes. They were playing tone pipes.

Owyn tugged on Lyf's sleeve, pointed at the draclings. "Look!"

They were still, strangely still. They stared up at the bluff with blank, fixed stares.

Tranced.

"Beat on the pots!" Lyf shouted. "Make a din!"

The children picked up pots and pans, tongs and spits,

weeding hooks and knives. They all began to beat. Owyn looked jubilant. His mouth formed little *booms,* but Lyf could not hear him, could hear nothing beyond the clangorous din. Her ears ached from it, but she didn't care.

The draclings blinked, looked alertly about. The pipe sounds were drowned out.

As they neared the cave, bolts rained down from the cliff, dimpling the water near their boat. And still the soldiers descended on their ropes. One got a foothold on the bottom lip of the cave. Lyf could see him opening his mouth to shout, but she couldn't hear his voice.

Couldn't hear . . .

Perhaps they weren't near enough the cave, and the tone pipes still penetrated through the din to trance the mother dragon. Or maybe she had flown. . . .

Where was Kaeldra? Where was Jeorg?

Their plan hadn't worked. All was lost. Lyf knew it. Lost. Unless . . .

"Scream!" she shouted. "We need to be louder. Scream!"

They did, then—all of them. Piercingly. The din was so fierce that Lyf clapped her hands over her ears, screaming all the while.

And then . . . a new sound. It started low, so that it seemed at first but a trembling in her bones. But it rose and rose to a bellowing roar. Rocks cascaded in runnels down the sides of the cliffs. The soldiers on their ropes seemed to freeze.

The dragon burst from the cave, streaming flame and smoke. She shot across the water, skimming the waves. She was longer than three fishing boats set end to end, greener than an emerald stone. Another roar: a scorching ball of blue flame tumbled across the waves and sizzled past their bow.

Lyf reached with her mind to touch the dragon but quickly pulled back. It was painful, painful like a crash of blinding-hot lightning against her skull.

The dragon spiraled up into the sky, rousing blustery wind gusts that tore at the sails and whipped the sea into a froth. The boat heeled over—hard. The screams broke off—all but Spens's. He yelled, pointing up at the sails, but the boat was tipping, tipping. Lyf was sliding across the wet deck with the mass of children and draclings—sliding toward the sea. Pots and pans went bouncing by. Just below, water gushed in a smooth green curve over the side of the boat.

"Reef the sail!" Spens shouted.

The boat slowly righted. Lyf took up a pot and bailed.

But now, through the rush of wind and wave, she heard the thin, shrill sound of the pipes. Lyf looked up to see soldiers on the cliff directly above. The dragon seemed to stall in the air. Slowly, she began to sink. Her fierce, slotted eyes glazed over. Her massive talons went limp. Wind fluttered in the slack, glittering folds of her wings.

A volley of bolts arced over the water, narrowly missing the dragon's tail.

"Beat the pots!" Lyf yelled. "Scream!" The children roused as if *they* had been tranced, and started up the din again.

Another volley of bolts. One struck the glittery stuff of the dragon's wing. A roar: the dragon lashed her tail, seemed to gather into herself, then soared up over the cliff, spewing flame. The soldiers scattered; the ropes were loosed; the cliff-hanging figures plummeted into the sea.

The dragon wafted just above the cave mouth. Air shimmered in the heat of her breath. Lyf could sense a summoning, a deep, compelling *thrum*. Though others kept up with the din, Lyf ceased with it and simply stared.

Something streaked out of the cave and came to drift in the air near the dragon. A dracling! Then another streaked out, and another, and another.

The mother dragon skimmed above the water toward the boat. Tatters of wingstuff fluttered where the bolt had gone through. Her draclings followed, glided in teetery arcs about her. Birds had gathered, Lyf saw. The sky was thick with clouds of wheeling seabirds.

The dragon, hovering, looked squarely down into their boat. Lyf shrank from the fierce heat of her gaze. The dragon sculled the air with her wings; wind gusted in Lyf's ears. She was summoning again—Lyf could feel it. Once more, Lyf tried to touch the dragon mind. Once more, she recoiled.

Bright.

Too bright and hot to touch.

All around her, audible above the din only by the rumbling in Lyf's bones, the draclings began to thrum.

Gently, Lyf reached into the carrier, cupped the hatchling's bony body in her hands, and held it up for the big green dragon to see. The dragon snorted out a twist of blue smoke and floated down so near that Lyf could taste the scorched, sulfury stench of her breath, so near that she could see herself mirrored in the curve of the dragon's huge eyes. Lyf held still, still, as talons long as daggers clutched round the little hatchling. A whuff of hot wind; the dragon slowly rose.

The hatchling was crying. Lyf could scarcely hear it through the din, but she *felt* the shrill, keening cry, and it twisted inside her. She blinked back tears, minding what Lunedweth had said: This wee one thinks you're its mam.

But I'm not, she thought. *I couldn't raise it. No one could—save for another dragon.*

You've a real mother now, little one.

Movement on the bluff. Some of the soldiers were returning.

<Go!> Lyf urged the draclings. <Go!>

Kindle leapt onto her shoulder; Lyf could feel the talons piercing her skin.

She looked at Skorch. <Go!> she commanded. If he would go, the others would likely follow.

Skorch turned to gaze at the hovering dragon. And now it came stronger, the summoning—came deep and warm and compelling.

"Tell them to go—and quickly!" Spens yelled in Lyf's ear. He was pointing at something; she turned to look.

A boat. Its sail was down, but the men within plied oars. It was closing in fast.

<Go, Skorch! You have to leave me. *She's* your mother now.>

The dracling didn't budge.

They'll never go, Lyf thought. *They'll never leave me. They'll all be killed.*

Skorch turned, then, looked long into Lyf's eyes. <Go,> she willed. <You must.> He puffed up, bobbled slowly into the air. One by one the other draclings followed: Smoak and the fierce-looking female with the high-arching ridges, the clumsy mottled green one and the chubby reddish one—all of them, save for Kindle. They rose in the air awkwardly with vellum-thin wings, but managed to stay afloat. The mother dragon dipped down to greet them, smooth as a rippling stream. She nuzzled them all over, with a low thrum in her throat that vibrated in Lyf's bones. Lyf wondered how they would fare on their long journey. They had flown so little, and this place where they were going was far. She wondered if the hatchling could manage so far without food. But . . . it was out of her hands now. They were *cared for* at last.

A bolt arced down from the bluff, splashed into the water near the boat.

The dragon, still clutching the hatchling, began to circle up into the sky. The draclings fluttered behind. They were out of reach of arrows now—all but Kindle.

<Go!> Lyf ordered Kindle. She tried to pluck the little dracling from her shoulders, but Kindle dug her talons hard into Lyf's flesh, all the while thrumming and nuzzling Lyf's face.

<Go! You *must!* Go!>

The boat tipped. Lyf saw that they were boarding, the men from the oared boat. There was a flash of knives; they were wresting the pots from the children. They were coming for her—for Kindle.

"Make her go!" Spens shouted.

<Kindle, *go!*> Lyf willed, but Kindle did not, and now Lyf knew that she never would.

A man was grappling with Spens, and Spens could not hold him off. They would kill Kindle if they caught her—that was sure.

Lyf could think of but one thing to do.

She looked up and fastened her gaze on a single, circling gull. She sent her mind up into it, felt Kindle release. The sea dropped away below and she was swimming on the wind with Kindle beside her, with draclings all around. Birds wheeled through liquid streams of air, the sharp high sounds of their cries mingling with the roar of dragon breath and the faraway squallings of men. Smells welled up, engulfed her: dragon feather salt fish water earth man. Far, far away, at the edges of the sea curve, something called to her. There was a lightness in her body. There was laughter in her bones.

Joy pulsed through her blood, swallowing up her words, swallowing up her thoughts, swallowing up her knowing of Lyf.

Harper's Tale

So. Lyf. You want me to tell of Lyf.

I will do so. Only . . .

Unless you've been living in a cave these many years past, you've heard before now that she sailed up the coast in a boatful of children and draclings, pursued by many hunters.

I won't weary you by telling of that.

You surely know as well of the soldiers and their tone pipes. Of how the children blocked the pipes' trancing of the dragons by beating on pots and pans. Of how the draclings flew across the sky with the last of the mother dragons.

All know of this. No need to dwell on the gaudy flash-and-glitter parts of a tale, as other harpers do.

So: back to Lyf.

She was gone, my lords and ladies.

She swooned when the last dracling left, and could not be roused.

They tried to bring her back—first Spens and Owyn and the other children in the boat, and then later Kaeldra and the harper and the fisherman in the cave. Lyf did not rouse even to smelling bitters. Didn't so much as blink.

Not dead, she was—not quite. She breathed, though shallowly. But gone she was, as surely as if she had been dead.

What of the soldiers, you ask? And the hunters?

You surprise me, lady, to break in on my telling of Lyf! You were so impatient to hear of her before.

But, since you ask . . .

When the deer are gone from the wood, my lords and ladies, the poachers take up their bows and go home.

To put it straightly: The prize was gone—the dragons. The queen's cause was lost, and the soldiers well knew it. Most skulked on back to Kragrom and pledged themselves to her cousin, the king (long may he live). Though some, charmed by the green hills of Elythia, stayed on, producing that widespread commingling of Elythian and Kragish blood that we see about us today. There were rumors that some soldiers had eaten of the hearts of draclings, and that metal could not bite their flesh. But when the king later put it to the test in a raid on Vittongal, many of them died. Perhaps the warding wore off. Perhaps it was but a fable.

The queen went into hiding. Some say she yet lives—though I know nothing of that.

The hunters? They were practical men, my lords. With none to pay a bounty, they hied themselves home to their wives.

Of Nysien, none have heard word. Some say he too went

with the soldiers and joined up with the king, though I count that unlikely. The life of a common soldier would not have suited him. In time he was given up for dead, and Mirym married another.

But back again to Lyf.

She slept, my lords and ladies.

She slept all the way to Merdoc in the fishing boat.

It was not a common sleep, but deeper. So deep you could not see her dreams flickering beneath her eyelids. So deep you could barely feel her pulse.

She did not eat. But when Kaeldra dripped water or gruel upon her lips, she sometimes swallowed.

They met up with Jeorg in Merdoc; his head was sore, but he was elsewise none the worse.

The children, once home, felt the weight of their parents' disapproval on their hind sides, and that was deemed penance enough. After, they were the centers of much wonderment as folk clamored to hear of their exploit.

Then the boy named Spens led them—Kaeldra, Jeorg, Owyn, the harper, and Lyf, (still sleeping)—to a healer he knew in the marshes north of Tyneth.

Lunedweth—enchanting creature! No sooner had the harper shared a cup of plum wine with her than he fell crown over boots in love. They've been wed these thirty years past, and she grows more beautiful day by day. (Though in truth, her cooking leaves something to be desired.) For I was that harper—now it can be told.

You knew it all along, my lass? Ah, but you're the clever one!

Yet even Lunedweth, with all her art, could not bring Lyf back.

I traveled on with the band of friends to the inn at Tyneth. All was somber there. The innkeeper's sister had been drowned not a septnight since. He was sick with grieving and would take no lodgers, would serve no meals. When Owyn heard of the drowning he began to weep, and neither his mama nor his da could comfort him.

And so at last we returned to the cottage in the hills of Elythia. Lyf's mother wept over her. Granmyr plied Lyf with herbs and chants and potions. Kaeldra, thinking to reach Lyf by means of a sorcery she performed with a potting wheel, spun clay until her hands were cracked and raw. But there was no magic in it.

And still Lyf slept. The moon turned and turned again, then turned two times more. And still she slept.

She grew thin, my lords and ladies. Wasting thin.

We feared she would never wake.

Fetch me another brew, lass, and bring me a stool. My feet are aching sore, and I can't bear to tell the next part standing.

Chapter 19

Deep Dream

In the deep, deep dream where she was living, she soared over the wrinkled waters to a cave thick with warm white mists. The Ancient Ones thronged within, filling the air with wing-stir and smolder-breath, filling her blood with thrummings. Their names eddied in and out of her knowing, like smoke.

Smoak. That was one of them. Other names crackled and hissed: Kindle. Skorch. Some names rumbled in her bones: Embyr. Byrn. There was a hatchling, ever near, and one who was always hungry.

What was his name?

It ebbed away from her. Came drifting back.

Pyro.

Yet something tugged at her, something she must remember, another life that floated beyond the dream. Sometimes she caught glimpses of it, echoes. A song. A face. A name. They wafted by. She couldn't catch them.

Remember.

In time, the tug of that other life thinned and melted away, like mist in the afternoon sun.

But now the earth was shifting in its sleep, was heeling over onto its side. Its breath grew chill. Birds poured past—calling, draining out of the sky.

Her own wings itched to fly.

Back across the waters. Wind-swimming: joy.

As land crept over the curved sea below, the tugging pulled at her again.

Remember. Try to remember.

And now she could taste it on the wind: the scent of a place she once knew.

And now she could hear it in the spaces between her bloodbeats: the murmur of voices beloved.

And now she could see it before her: the fold in the green-gold hills.

These hills.

This fold.

Here.

She must go here.

Harper's Tale

Autumn comes glorious to the hills of Elythia, my lords and ladies—crisp and tart and golden as a new-picked apple. The wild pansies bloom, and a brisk, teasing wind scrapes the mist from the face of the sky.

Alas, all too soon the season bares its bitter edge. The skies go gray and sullen; the wind turns cruel and bites. It rips great clumps of thatch from cottage and byre. It rages in the blackthorns, spitting out leaves and twigs and branches, strewing the wreckage of blasted gardens all about the graze.

Birds thread across the sky in long processions, heading south.

It was on such a morning that Kaeldra found herself alone in Granmyr's cottage. Alone . . . save for Lyf, who lay yet unmoving on her pallet. Owyn was helping his da mend the byre thatch; Lyska and Aryanna were with Granmyr and Lyf's mother, scavenging the last of the herbs from the wind-razed kitchen garden.

Kaeldra was grown large with child and could not well lift or climb or stoop to toilsome work. Others must do that for her. But weaving—that she could do. And keep watch on Lyf.

She had just stood to stretch the kinks out of her back, when there came a loud thump at the shutters.

(I do not hatch this tale from fancy, my ladies. I tell it to you just as Kaeldra told it to me.)

"Who's there?" she asked, thinking it strange that someone would knock. Why didn't they enter? The door was closed, but not latched.

No reply.

Kaeldra moved to the shutters, opened them a crack, peered out.

Nothing.

That was odd, she thought.

She closed the shutters and had just turned back to the loom when the sound came again:

Thump!

And then *thump!*

And *thump!* yet again.

A prickling chill crept up her spine, lifted the hair on her scalp. She moved swiftly to the shutters, flung them wide. Something streaked through the window, into the room.

A gull.

It circled once, circled twice, circled three times round—like *so*, my lords and ladies.

It lit down upon Lyf's chest.

It stared straight into her sleeping face and cocked its head to one side.

Kaeldra froze. Watched. Did not dare to breathe.

The gull shook itself, let out a startled cry. And then it was flying out the window; it was gone.

Kaeldra turned to gaze after. She watched until it shrank to a small, pale speck, until it vanished in the sky. She was filled with a sudden sharp sorrow, though she didn't know quite why, or for what she had hoped.

The voice took her by surprise. Lyf's voice.

"Kaeldra? Is it you?"

And so my tale is done, my lords and ladies. If it has pleased you, would you be so kind as to toss a coin or two into this hat for a poor old harper? Copper is fine, but silver is better. (And a slab of venison would not go amiss.) Generosity, my lords, is as much a virtue as patience. Nay, more! And—

What say you, my lord? What happened *next*?

Why, nothing—out of the common way of things. Lyf woke—that's all you need to know. The details of contented lives make but meager grist for tales, my lord.

Did Lyf get well, you ask, my lady?

In time. All came to her in time.

What? Marriage, you ask?

My lady! My tale is done! Must *every* tale treat with love and marriage? Ah, but if it will loose the coins from that purse of yours, I will tell you this: Spens of Merdoc took her for his bride. In time.

She has led a common life, my lords and ladies. She no longer kens with birds—she cannot. That's gone, along with the Ancient Ones. Gone for good. All the old magic is gone . . . save for in her dreams.

She yet has wondrous dreams.

Pronunciation Guide

Since so many people have asked me how to pronounce the proper names in *Dragon's Milk* and *Flight of the Dragon Kyn*, I thought I'd show how I pronounce the names in this book. However, you have my permission to say them any way that feels comfortable to you!

—Susan Fletcher

Lyf's Family

Aryanna (ä´rē-ä´nə)
Granmyr (grăn´mîr)
Jeorg (jā´ōrg)
Kaeldra (kāl´drə)
Lyf (lĭf)
Lyska (lĭs´kə)
Mirym (mîr´yəm)
Nysien (nĭs´yĕn)
Owyn (ō´wĭn)

Other Characters

Alys (ä´lēz)
Aura (ôr´ə)
Brita (brĭt´ə)
Brynn (brĭn)
Cletus (klē´təs)
Donal (dŭn´əl)
Dwynn (dwĭn)
Galum (gă´lŭm)
Gar (gär)
Kymo (kī´mō)

Lunedweth (lo͞on´əd-wĕth´)
Spens (spĕnz)
Turi (tûr´ē)
Una (o͞on´ə)
Yanil (yän´əl)

Dragons and Draclings (drăk´lĭngs)
Byrn (bûrn)
Embyr (ĕm´bər)
Kindle (kĭnd´l)
Pyro (pi´rō)
Skorch (skôrch)
Smoak (smōk)

Places
Elythia (əl-ĭth´ē-ə´)
Kragrom (krăg´räm)
Merdoc (mâr´däk)
Tyneth (tin´əth)
Vittongal (vĭt´tŏn-gäl´)
Wyrmward (wûrm´wôrd)

Background Events

(for *Flight of the Dragon Kyn*, *Dragon's Milk*, and *Sign of the Dove*)

YEAR	EVENT
1*	Clutch "a" laid**
78	Clutch "b" laid
102	Kara born
99-106	Clutch "a" hatched
109	Landerath born
112	Granmyr born
117	The Migration
121	Kara's daughter born
141	Kara's granddaughter born (Kaeldra's mother)
	Kara's daughter dies in childbirth
146	Ryfenn (Lyf's mother) born
155	Clutch "c" laid in land of exile?
160	Kaeldra born
164	Kara dies
	Kaeldra and her mother flee Kragrom
	Mirym born
165	Kaeldra and her mother arrive in Elythia
	Kaeldra's mother dies
171	Lyf born
174	Bryam (Lyf's father) dies
176	First hatchings from clutch "b"
	Kaeldra takes first draclings away
183	Last hatchings from clutch "b"

*Assigning the number one to this year is purely arbitrary.

**Dragon eggs incubate for 98-105 years; they are laid every 77 years. The hatching cycle lasts up to seven years.

Here's a peek at the long-awaited fourth volume of Susan Fletcher's Dragon Chronicles

PART I

EGG

Something old,
Something new,
Something broken,
Someone blue.

What was whole
Has come undone.
Something's broken,
Someone's blue.

—From "Broken & Blue" by White Raven

† † †

Mercury and PCBs,
Nitrogen dioxide,
Arsenic and desert dust
Blotting out the sun.

Breathe in.
Breathe it all in:
Now you and the celumbra are one.

—From "Sky Shadow" by Mutant Tide

PLEATHER

Back in the house, I put everything away—coat, boots, flashlight. I kenned Stella down to my shoulder and was heading upstairs when I all-at-once froze, halfway freaking out Stella, who lurched forward on my shoulder, flapped her wings for balance, and about poked out my eye with a feather.

There was Piper on the landing—rumpled nightie, ducky slippers, round glasses too big for her five-year-old face. Sitting there. Watching.

"What are you doing up?" I kept my voice quiet. Aunt Pen was a sound sleeper. Once the hearing aid came out she was gone: out for the night. Still, better not push it. Aunt Pen would fry a circuit if she saw Stella uncaged.

"Looking for you," Piper said.

"Well, I'm here now. Get back to bed. We'll both go back to bed."

"Will you catch Luna?"

"Luna! Did you let her out?"

Piper shrugged.

I groaned. Inside, though—not out loud. I'd look pretty stupid getting on her case about Luna, with Stella sitting right there on my shoulder.

"Where is she?" I asked.

"In the basement."

"The basement!" I remembered Aunt Pen and took it down a notch. "How did that happen?"

"I was looking for you. And I opened the basement door and she flew down."

"Did you try to ken her back?"

Piper nodded. "She wouldn't come!" Her voice spiked up: high-megahertz whine.

"Shh!" I put my arm around her. She leaned against me, buried her face in my shirt. "Hey. It's okay." It actually takes years to get kenning worked out with your bird—no matter how talented you are. It's more complicated than you might think, and Piper'd had Luna for less than a year. Luna: as in *Stellaluna*, our favorite picture-book bat.

I might be able to summon Luna myself, but it's not the done thing to ken another person's bird. It's just not polite.

A thought struck me. The basement.

I held Piper's shoulders and pushed her away so I could see her face. "Why did you open the basement door? Did you hear something down there?"

"No."

"Sort of a thumping sound?"

"No! I was just looking."

Okay. I breathed. Okay. "Did you see where she went?"

"It was dark. And I couldn't reach the switch."

Don't wanna.

I *so* wished I could leave this till morning. But no way would Piper go to sleep without Luna.

"You wait here," I said.

I fumbled for the light switch just inside the

basement door. Way down below, the ancient fixture clicked on—buzzing, flickering, and dim. I peered into the shadows. No sign of Luna. Ditzy bird. I started down the steps, breathing in *eau de basement*—metallic-smelling, sort of, mixed with chemicals and dust. Halfway to the bottom, Stella pushed off my shoulder and glided past the sputtery light, into the shadows.

"Hey," I said.

I tried summoning her, but she slipped away. I could feel her faintly farther back, but she was dissing me.

Bad bird. Bad, bad bird.

I heard a scratching sound as Stella lit down someplace I couldn't see, then a little greeting *peep* from Luna.

I hesitated on the bottom step and scanned the room. Hadn't been down here in years. There was the furnace. The lawn furniture, stacked and covered, waiting for spring. The banks of floor-to-ceiling shelves with their neat plastic bins, all neatly labeled and color-coded, Aunt Pen style.

HOLIDAY DECORATIONS. PAPER PRODUCTS. CLEANING SUPPLIES. LIGHT BULBS. STYROFOAM PACKING PEANUTS.

No Stella. No Luna. At least, not that I could see.

I moved past the first bank of shelves, then deeper back, past the next. PAINT. CARPET REMNANTS. EBAY. GOODWILL. There were a couple of plastic bins labeled DAMAGED FIGURINES—a tidy little graveyard for those bloodless birds of hers. Birds that didn't shed feathers or strew seeds. Birds that didn't poop.

The furnace snicked on, grumbled to life. A draft stirred the cobwebs at the tops of the shelves. I wished I'd put on my flip-flops. The concrete was seismic frigid, and bits of grit clung to the bottoms of my feet.

Ahead, at the far, dim end of the room, six or seven beat-up cardboard boxes sat in a heap on the floor. They looked so different from Aunt Pen's pristine plastic bins, I knew what they must be.

The ones Dad had sent last week. The ones

he'd found in that storage locker in Alaska. Full of Mom's research stuff, he said.

We'd never even known about the locker until the overdue notice came. They were going to "dispose of the contents" unless someone paid, like pronto. So Dad went right back up to Anchorage, hoping to find some clues.

And there, at the top of the pile of boxes, were Stella and Luna. One each: cockatiel and canary. They seemed to be staring down into the narrow space between the boxes and the shelves. Ignoring me completely.

Could they smell Mom, maybe? Was that why they'd come down here?

I crept up behind Luna, pressed a finger against the backs of her twiggy legs. She lifted one foot and seemed about to fall for it—to step back onto my finger—but at the last second she tumbled to my nefarious plan and fluttered up to the top of the shelves.

"Twit," I muttered.

The box, I saw, was marked up and tattered,

having spent its previous life shipping ink cartridges from Taiwan. I strained to decipher the tiny postmark in the stuttering light. ANCHORAGE, AK.

I ran my fingers across Dad's handwriting—the careful, rounded letters, the hopeful upward dips at the ends of words. *Soon,* he'd said when he'd called earlier this evening. He would come home soon.

When is soon? I'd asked. It was nearly two weeks already. But he couldn't answer that. Had he found anything, any clues? *Too soon to tell,* he'd said.

I sighed, feeling the old familiar ache hollowing out my insides.

"Bryn?"

I turned around. Piper was leaning into the doorway at the top of the stairs.

"Bryn, did you find her?" She sounded a little wheezy.

"Yes. I'll be there soon." I heard the echo: *Soon.*

"With Luna?"

"Yes. In a minute. Go get your inhaler, would you?"

I looked where the birds were staring and saw that one of the boxes seemed to have tipped off the stack and landed on the floor on its side. The flaps had popped open; little clumps of wadded newspaper spilled out across the concrete, behind the other stacked boxes, beneath the lowest shelf.

A shiver brushed the back of my neck. Something had happened here. But what?

I synched with Stella and felt a weird, restless energy. Curiosity—on steroids. Something drawing her in.

I squatted beside the tipped box. It had been closed up with that brown paper sealing tape—not the stronger, plastic stuff you're supposed to use for mailing. It looked as if the glue had come ungummed, and then the tape had torn.

It was mostly dirt samples in the boxes, Dad had said. Dirt with microbes in it. Bugs, Mom called them. She was always looking for promising new bugs. Bugs that would eat toxic waste. Dad had sent half the samples to Taj at the lab and half here, just to be safe.

I righted the box, set it on the floor beside the other ones. I raked through the crumpled paper inside. Nothing. I peered beneath the shelf, following the trail of newsprint.

Something there. Roundish. Hard to see way back there in the shadows.

A soccer ball? A volleyball?

From here, it looked kind of like leather, but it wouldn't have to be. It could be that plastic synth leather. Pleather. It seemed to have sections, sort of, like crocodile skin or a tortoise shell. And it wasn't quite round. More ovalish.

An egg? Some kind of mega-huge egg?

Ostrich?

Emu?

Whatever it was, it definitely wasn't dirt.

"What are you into, Mom?" I murmured.

Luna fluttered down again, beside Stella.

Both of them still fixated on that egg. "Hate to break it to you, ladies," I said, "but this is way out of your league."

Maybe, when the egg had rolled out of the box, it had bumped the wooden post that held up the shelves. Ergo the mysterious thumps.

Maybe. But wouldn't that happen just once?

"Bryn?" Piper again. "Are you coming?"

"Soon! Just wait there."

I got down on my hands and knees, reached way back beneath the shelf. I touched the egg. It gave a little, like a rubber ball. I scooted forward, stretched full-out on the floor, and gently cupped my whole hand over it.

Weird. It was maybe a teensy bit warmer against my palm than it should have been. Not very warm, but it was chilly down here. You'd think the egg would be too.

And something else. It had a funny kind of vibe to it. So faint, I almost couldn't tell if I was imagining it. But I didn't think I was.

All at once, sprawled out there in the dark,

with so many mysteries bumping around in my head . . . all at once, I knew one small thing for absolute certain.

Whatever it was inside this egg, it was *alive.*

On the trail of a squeal and a squeak,

Isabelle Bean opens a door . . . falls through the opening . . . and tumbles into a very different world, right into the middle of a wild adventure. There are frightened children who are convinced she is an evil witch. Her grandma might actually *be* a witch. This new world is very strange and exciting, and Isabelle can't wait to take it all in. But just what is Isabelle doing there—and will she ever get home?